The Prince's Secret

El-Mitra Family

Elizabeth Lennox

ISBN13: 9798375886312

Table of Contents

Chapter 1

Emma groaned, glaring at the empty tea kettle. "Seriously?"

Her sleepy glare turned to the empty, silent hallway. But Amanda, Emma's roommate and best friend, wasn't awake yet, so her best friend wasn't aware of the caffeine-induced antipathy directed towards her.

With a sigh, Emma grumpily padded over to the sink to re-fill the electric kettle, stopping her brain from thinking that the kettle was laughing at her. "Just a kettle," she hissed as the water poured into the kettle.

Every night, she filled the kettle so that she only needed to flip the switch at the bottom to start the heating process. Most mornings, it wasn't an issue. But every once in a while, her roommate engaged in a late night writing binge to meet her deadlines and guzzled coffee to help her concentrate.

Amanda was Emma's best friend, so she tried to be forgiving. But messing with one's morning caffeine fix? That was cruel and unusual punishment in roommate protocols.

Sighing with resignation, Emma settled the beaten up electric kettle onto the heating stand and flipped the switch to begin the heating process. Once she had the water started, Emma meandered over to her computer to see the latest news headlines. With a satisfied smile, Emma read the top headline, her shoulders relaxing as a warm sense of success welled up within her.

The headline today was her story. She'd done that! She'd revealed the senator's multiple illegal stock transfers. She'd even quoted his previous declarations about how all politicians needed to rise higher in their moral integrity in order to preserve the virtue of their office and demonstrate that the public could trust their leaders. It was hard to trust someone who was able to increase their net worth into the millions in just a few years when raking in a salary of only low six figures.

Emma emitted an inelegant snort as she shuffled in her bunny-slip-pered feet to the shower. "Time to start the day," she muttered, pushing sleep-crazed hair out of her face. Emma was not a sound sleeper! She tossed and turned every night, her mind going too fast to let her truly relax. She had to be seriously exhausted for her body to finally give in and sleep. And even then, if she was able to get six hours of sleep, life was wonderfully delicious that day! Eight hours of sleep? Emma snorted again as she turned on the hot water in the shower. Never hap-pened!

Fifteen minutes later, showered and dressed, her still-wet hair pulled up into a messy bun, Emma poured the hot water from the kettle into the French press. "Five minutes," she whispered to no one. "Just five more minutes and I will..."

She froze, staring at the laptop. Her headline, the top headline that she was so proud of...was gone! In this time of whiplash technology, the news cycles were by the moment instead of twenty-four hours. This new headline was replaced by...!

"Are you kidding me?" she whispered, rushing across the room and almost missing her chair entirely as she dropped into the seat, glaring at the newest headline. "Forced vasectomies for prisoners?" she read out loud. "That's...inhumane!"

"What's wrong?" Amanda asked, padding into the room in her fluffy, pink slippers. She held a cup of tea, but Emma didn't think to admon-ish her roommate for stealing the hot water again. This newest, outra-geous headline took up all of her mind-space.

Emma shook her head in stunned horror as she read, "Our esteemed governor has proposed legislation that would require all current crimi-nals held in the prison system to undergo a vasectomy!"

Amanda's eyes widened, her cup of tea halted halfway to her mouth. "Are you kidding me?" she hissed, moving forward as if to read the headline herself.

Emma didn't bother to answer, correctly assuming her friend's ques-tion was rhetorical. She scrolled through the article, skimming the words quickly. "According to one of my sources," she paused and glanced meaningfully at Amanda, as they rolled their eyes in unison, "during a press conference late last night, the governor claimed that the prisoners, with no exceptions, should undergo the sterilization proce-dure in order to protect the next generation from...!"

Amanda's horrified voice picked up where Emma broke off. "...The potential insanity that he's recognized in the criminal population!" Amanda finished, reading the same article on her cell phone. "The governor truly believes that the prison inmates are insane?" She braced a hand on the desk. "He thinks that every prisoner should endure a vasectomy in order to halt the genetic makeup from being passed on to future generations?"

"I just...!" Emma didn't realize that her mouth was still hanging open as she continued to scroll through the rest of the article. "What in the world?" she whispered. "Is there a new study that came out from some pseudo-doctor claiming that the prison population was...?"

Amanda's hand fell to her lap as they stared at each other. "This is awful!" Emma whispered. "Prisoners aren't insane! They committed a crime! Some of them have learning disabilities! Some were abused as children and violence is all that they understand!"

Amanda nodded. "I agree!" She lifted her phone and found the "Flipper" icon, the latest app that compiled headlines from several different news sources. "This crazy headline is blowing up all over social media." She scrolled through the postings and shook her head in disbelief. "Everyone is livid about the idea."

Emma sighed and leaned back against the leather chair. A moment later, she stood up and pushed the plunger through the coffee grounds of her beloved French press, then poured herself a cup of fragrant coffee.

She leaned against the kitchen countertop, her mind whirling. She took a sip of coffee, trying to figure out why a governor would recommend such a controversial idea. "Do you really think so?" Emma asked.

Amanda blinked. "You don't?"

Emma stared at the wall, not really seeing the dents and marks on the old drywall. "It sounds...too...outrageous."

Amanda shrugged as she sipped her tea. "That governor has announced some pretty crazy ideas lately." She took another sip of her tea, contemplating the problem. "It's almost as if someone sits in a closet somewhere and tries to think up the most controversial idea just to get their name into the news."

Emma blew on the steaming coffee, nodding in agreement. "He's definitely come up with some crazy, non-sensical ideas," she replied and took a sip of her coffee. She glanced at the headline again, her head tilting as she considered her roommate's point. "I think you might have a point. This is too crazy. Too controversial." One of her fingers tapped an erratic beat against the side of her coffee mug. Emma still stared at the wall, but her mind was whirling. "This *has* to be a publicity stunt. And I think you pointed out the issue. This guy is most likely trying to get his name into the headlines again since he's obviously trying to position himself for a future run for president."

Amanda's hand fell onto her lap and she snorted, her body language just as elegant as Emma. "You think he's not really going to sterilize prisoners? You think the governor is merely tossing this idea out into the internet as a publicity stunt?" She tilted her head slightly, considering that idea. "But I don't understand the tactic. Seriously, who would vote for someone with that type of statement on his record?"

Emma took another long sip of her coffee as she shrugged dismissively. "A lot of people who are big on anti-crime, I'm guessing."

Amanda shifted slightly, still shaking her head. "I don't like it. Even if it's just a publicity stunt, comments like that are dangerous."

Emma nodded, her mind still intently focused. "I agree with you, but thankfully, I doubt that the state senate and house will allow something that crazy to pass. I doubt that it's even legal. It sounds like cruel and unusual punishment to me." She turned and started typing. "Besides, I..." Emma's voice trailed off as her mind reeled with the possibilities.

The sounds of typing filled the room and Amanda smiled at her friend. Emma had thought of something and her mind was now going down that rabbit hole.

There was a long silence and Amanda watched her friend, amused and impressed with Emma's ability to concentrate so completely. Suddenly, Emma's fingers flew over the keyboard as an idea occurred to her.

Emma started typing up a response to the article about the forced vasectomies, but then stopped and considered the idea from a different angle. What if...? No, that wasn't possible. Or was it? Quickly, she pulled up a webpage, her eyes skimming over the information. She wrote something down on the notepad she kept beside her laptop, then tapped her pen against the side of her head. Pulling up another website, Emma wondered if the governor had somehow looked back in history and...? She made notes on legal issues to research and people who might give her a bit of insight or a quote that would explain the governor's action.

However, a moment later, Amanda interrupted Emma's thoughts on her next article, one that would blast the governor's suggestion.

Amanda asked hesitantly, "But...what if it *isn't?*"

Emma froze, her fingers poised above the keyboard. Then she did a double take. Amanda was standing in the middle of their small family room, the cup of tea cradled in her hands, staring at Emma with wide, concerned eyes.

"What if it isn't...what?" Emma prompted.

It took Amanda a moment to collect her thoughts. She licked her lips and started pacing. "What if it isn't...just a headline?" she whispered, turning wide eyes back to Emma.

Emma sipped her coffee and pointed to her laptop's screen. "But...it *is* a headline. And there's video of the governor announcing the initiative in a press conference."

Amanda rushed over, perching on the edge of the beat-up coffee table that they'd found on the side of the road and cleaned up. A free piece of furniture was a precious gift!

Leaning forward, she looked at Emma with an intensity that was usually reserved for her book plots. "What if it isn't *just* a headline?" She snapped her fingers in the air several times, looking around as if distracted. "What was that movie? Something about...a wagging dog?"

Emma shrugged one shoulder and, with a chuckle, replied, "It was called 'Wag the Dog'. It was released back during that presidential scandal in the nineties, I think."

Amanda nodded. "Yeah! That one." She leaned forward a bit more. "What if *that*," she pointed to the headline still on Emma's screen, "is *more* than just a crazy headline?"

Emma blinked, frowned at the headline, then gazed back at Amanda. Her voice was low, almost awed, as understanding came to her. "You think that this announcement by a previously unknown politician isn't just a way for him to gain national attention?"

Amanda nodded slowly, almost unconsciously sipping her tea. There was a sparkle of understanding in her blue eyes now. "I don't know," she whispered back. With a grin, she jerked her chin towards Emma. "Why don't you do a bit of digging?"

Amanda stood up and moved towards the hallway. "I bet there's a whole lot more to the story than just a crazy idea from a governor looking to get a bit of publicity," she called out over her shoulder.

A moment later, Emma heard the shower starting, but her thoughts were focused on the possibilities. Amanda was right. The idea of requiring all prisoners to undergo sterilization surgery was just too wild. She lifted her phone and scrolled through the posts on several social media sites. Sure enough, everyone was talking about the crazy suggestion, lambasting the proposal. Social media readers were livid that someone would suggest something so outrageous and inhumane, so disgustingly horrible!

Emma turned to her computer and started sifting through information. She pulled up the state's legislative agenda, going through the proposed bills currently moving through the house and senate. Nothing too wild there.

A toasted bagel with avocado appeared at her elbow and Emma absently took a bite. In the back of her mind, she vaguely heard the door to their apartment open and close, so Amanda must be heading off to work. But Emma remained focused on her research.

Amanda was right. Now that her friend had pointed out the possibility, Emma's gut told her that Amanda was right. Something odd was happening. Emma's fingers flew over the keyboard, her mind racing as she dug deep to discover the real issue behind the attention-grabbing headline.

Chapter 2

He shook his head and Prince Rayed's bodyguards immediately stepped forward, stopping the woman in the shimmering, barely-there pink dress from approaching him. She pouted slightly, giving him a credible puppy-dog gaze, but turned with a shrug and sauntered away, offering him a lovely view of her backside in the tight dress. Rayed suspected that she added a bit more swing to her hips than was strictly necessary, for his benefit. He stifled a sigh as he looked away, entirely uninterested.

But that begged the question; why the hell *wasn't* he interested? Why was he bored out of his mind by the parade of lovely ladies who tossed him subtle and not-so-subtle glances? There were about a dozen women here who were gorgeous and might distract him from the tedium that had become his life lately. Rayed knew that the ladies might only distract him for a night, but wouldn't that be enough?

No, it wasn't tedium, he thought as he took a sip of his martini. It was jealousy. Back home, Rayed constantly witnessed the happiness between his brother, Sheik Tazir, and his lovely wife, Lila. After a rocky, sometimes amusing start to their relationship, the two of them were madly in love and were now expecting their first child.

He didn't want that. Rayed knew that he wasn't ready for marriage and a family. He preferred his freedom and he definitely wasn't ready to become a father! So, why the hell was he jealous of his brother's joy? Why did he feel this simmering rage whenever he needed to return to Farhe for any reason? And yes, he was finding more and more excuses to be out of the country lately. The last time he'd been home, Rayed had endured the concerned glances from his sisters, Sada and Zhara, which had annoyed him further.

So here he was, standing in an elegant Philadelphia hotel ballroom, watching the elite of the Philadelphia society mingle, laugh, and pretend that they were having a wonderful time. Meanwhile, Rayed was wondering why he was here. Unfortunately, he couldn't go home. Farhe was...he loved his country. As the Economic Minister, Rayed was in charge of ensuring the economic success of both his family and his country. He loved business, loved finding ways to invest money and expand the prosperity of his people.

But going home meant seeing Tazir, adoring his wife, sending her tender, loving glances, touching her and seeing his gentle love returned in Lila's eyes.

It wasn't even that Tazir was pressuring Rayed to marry. Not in words, anyway. But since Rayed didn't have someone like Lila by his side, he couldn't stomach the idea of marriage.

"Your Highness," an older woman in yet another shimmering evening gown approached, her hand extended. Rayed gave the signal that she could approach. She was the hostess of this evening, after all. No need to offend her simply because Rayed was in a foul mood. The lady smiled brightly, shaking his hand. "It's such an honor that you chose to grace us with your presence tonight."

He dug deep and found a bit of charm. "I'm honored that you extended the invitation to me," he replied, knowing the words that were required in these sorts of social situations.

The woman beamed, her hand moving to her chest. "I can't tell you how excited we were when you stepped through the door!" she exclaimed, the diamond rings on her fingers sparkling off of the overhead light. "I'm sure that the number of donations to our precious charity will skyrocket now that you're here."

Charity? This was a charity event? Rayed smothered several epithets. He *hated* charity functions. Okay, he hated all social functions lately. The only satisfaction he seemed to experience these days was during a productive business transaction. Yes, business was fascinating, he thought. Social events? Why the hell did he keep attending these things? He hated them, found them boring and irritating!

With a mental sigh, he forced a polite smile as he listened. But in his mind, he was thinking that perhaps he should get out of here and just... focus on business. No more social engagements, no more smiling for the press and acting as if everything was fine.

The hostess continued to speak, but Rayed had tuned her out, although he managed to smile and nod in all the right places during the conversation.

"Muqadas!" he hissed.

Behind his blathering hostess, his eyes caught sight of a woman in a crimson, silk dress. The shimmering material skimmed over her luscious curves, leaving nothing to the imagination. Well, the material covered her skin from her shoulders to her toes, but...heaven help him! That dress was...and the woman in the dress? She was beyond lovely! Gleaming dark hair cascaded over her shoulders and...he could see her blue eyes from across the room, they were so bright and clear and... looking for someone?

Rayed was barely listening to his hostess drone on about...he had no idea what the woman was discussing. His thoughts were completely focused on the woman in red silk. She was slim, but with lush curves that his hands ached to explore. An errant thought about his brother's recent obsession with lipstick color popped into his head and his body instantly reacted.

"No," he grumbled.

"No?" the hostess echoed, clearly startled. He couldn't remember her name, much less whatever she'd been prattling on about.

Rayed pulled his eyes away from the woman in red, looking into the eyes of the offended older woman. Damn it, he hadn't been listening. Again!

Rayed forced a polite smile. "I apologize..." he couldn't remember her name so he didn't even try, "...I was distracted by another thought. Would you...?" he stopped speaking when the sultry, sexy beauty moved forward and...stumbled over the silk hem of her dress. Rayed barely restrained himself from laughing out loud when the mysterious beauty muttered something under her breath as she lifted the hem. Obviously that was not her dress, he thought. It was an expensive creation of shimmering red silk that enhanced her coloring perfectly, but it was too long. Any woman who could afford that dress would have had it hemmed.

Rayed didn't mind the woman's mis-step since, when she bent over to gather the hem, the action allowed him a brief glimpse of the soft curve of her luscious breasts. Not overly full, but not too small either. Perfect breasts. A C cup, he suspected. A handful, but not overflowing.

Again, he thought about his brother's conundrum about nipple color and lipstick. His older brother, Tazir, had overheard Lila talking with their sisters, Princess Sada and Princess Zhara, about choosing the perfect lip color. Apparently, there was a trend spiraling through social media that a woman's perfect lip color would be the same color as her nipples.

This woman's lips were red, the same shade as her dress. The color was a bit shocking against her dark hair and pale skin, but it looked perfect to him. But he didn't believe for a moment that her nipples were a matching shade. No, he suspected that the woman's nipples were...he had to stop thinking about the color of her nipples. His body was already responding to the delectable possibilities.

"I should introduce you to some people," his hostess was saying, even going so far as to look around for someone important enough to introduce him to.

"No need," he interjected, even touching her arm to stop her. "I'm fine right here."

The woman's mouth fell open, as if the idea of an important person being left alone was too outrageous and horrifying to contemplate. "Nonsense!" she insisted with a social laugh. She lifted a hand in the air and, immediately, several people in immaculate tuxedos separated themselves from their current group and moved towards her. "Good evening, Stella," one of the men greeted the hostess, finally giving Rayed the name that he had forgotten. "What mischief are you up to tonight?"

Stella chuckled, obviously flattered that some idiot in a tuxedo would think that she was up to anything other than improving her social status. "Oh you!" she said with a playful nudge at his arm. "George, I'd like to introduce you to..."

"Prince Rayed el Mitra of Fahre," George interrupted, extending his hand. "We were introduced at the Met Gala several years ago. Wonderful to see you again, Your Highness."

Stella laughed, delighted that she'd connected two people who could now talk about things that could potentially reshape the world. Or maybe reveal a few stock tips that she could call in to her stockbroker. Insider stock trading penalties were for others. Not for the wealthy. In fact, it was how more than ninety percent of the people in this room had built their wealth.

Rayed listened with half an ear as the men around him discussed something about a building that they wanted to tear down and replace with more modern structure. He wasn't sure which building, nor did he care. He was more focused on the woman as she carefully moved through the creatively decorated space. The black and white décor of tonight's gala was the perfect backdrop for the woman's red dress, even though she was standing back, obviously trying to remain in the shadows for some odd reason.

As he watched, Rayed noticed that the mystery woman kept a firm grip on her dress, her matching purse tucked securely under her arm, which made the "casual" sipping of champagne an issue.

She pulled out her cell phone, surreptitiously snapped a picture of one of the other guests and typed something, then sipped more champagne.

Correction, she pretended to sip the expensive sparkling wine. In reality, Rayed suspected that the liquid was merely touching her lips so that the woman in red looked as if she were participating in the social niceties. And yet, he instinctively knew that the lovely woman wasn't at this event in a social capacity.

Her phone must have buzzed because she glanced down at the screen. Her lips twisted into a grimace. Instantly, Rayed was curious about what the reply had said.

She looked around, apparently spotted someone else, took another picture, then typed in another message. Moments later, she read another message and sighed with impatience. Rayed swallowed a chuckle at her frustration, but he didn't want the other men to notice her. The red dress was enough of a lure, but if they actually noticed the woman, there would be a hoard of men vying for her attention.

Not to mention, he wanted to know what was going on with the pictures and the messages. Whatever her plan, it didn't seem to be working.

He was fascinated!

Emma wished that she hadn't worn this particular dress. Amanda had loaned it to her and her roommate was taller by a couple of inches. That meant that the dress was just a little too long, so Emma kept tripping on the hem. And the shoes? Dear heaven, the heels that Amanda had forced Emma to wear were way too high! Emma usually wore sturdy boots or even sneakers, since she walked a lot during her efforts to capture a news story. Plus, these torture devices on her feet had one strap over her toes and one behind her ankle. They looked stunning, but there was nothing else holding the stupid shoe to her foot. Plus, were there needles on the bottom? Maybe that was why her feet were killing her and she'd only been standing here in this stupid hotel ballroom for less than twenty minutes.

After smothering another groan, she found one more man that looked promising.

She snapped another picture of the guy, then sent it off to Amanda and waited. She pretended to sip the champagne. She didn't want to get drunk. Tonight was too important. Plus, the stupid purse under her arm was quickly becoming more than just an annoyance. When she worked, she normally had a hefty backpack that was securely strapped to both of her shoulders. A backpack was significantly more useful than a tiny, red clutch that only had room for her driver's license, a credit card, and a tube of lipstick. Seriously, why would anyone use this purse?

While she waited for Amanda to come back with information, she spotted her prey. Governor Mitchell was here! He was schmoozing with various other guests, none of whom Emma recognized. But she snapped pictures of the man and anyone he spoke with. She'd discover their identities later.

Governor Mitchell being here meant that her plan just might work! However, getting an invitation to this party had been a fluke. Getting into all of the other parties happening over the next few days would be a harder achievement.

"Give me someone!" she impatiently texted. Amanda was back at their apartment searching the internet for facial images and information. Emma took the picture then sent the image to Amanda. Her friend would then look up the person's name on the internet. So far, she'd sent Amanda five pictures of men who might be a good candidate for her plan. But Amanda had rejected all of them.

There was one man, a dark haired, tanned Adonis that was standing off to the side. She could feel his eyes on her, but refused to glance in his direction. He wouldn't work for their plan. He was too tall, too scary looking, and too...smart. Yes, the guy didn't look like the kind who would fall for her act. She needed someone a bit more...persuasive for this to work.

After three more images were taken and rejected, Emma decided that she needed to circulate through the room. Plus, she suspected there was a pebble in her shoe! How there could actually be a pebble in her shoe when there wasn't much shoe to hold anything, not even her feet, Emma wasn't sure.

Stepping away from the high-top table behind which she'd been "hiding", Emma turned and...almost ran into the intimidating stranger she'd been avoiding for the past hour. The man was tall, handsome, and impossibly attractive. Plus, there was something about him that screamed "power!". That was a sensation she didn't need. Not for her plan to work.

Tilting her head way back, she stared up into the stranger's eyes. He had sharp, well defined features. Hard and intense eyes, hawk-like nose, and granite jawline.

Had she added "terrifying" to that list of adjectives? If she hadn't Emma added it now. Because the man was absolutely terrifying! Emma could see the intelligence shining in his eyes. And curiosity!

Nope! Curiosity was a bad thing. In her experience, men were generally pretty oblivious to anything that didn't pertain to their own comfort and desires. They definitely weren't curious about something that wasn't within their personal sphere. So curiosity was a no-go in the kind of person she was looking for at this moment. No, this particular man might be fascinating and intelligent, but he definitely wasn't a good choice for her plan.

However, because she didn't want to be kicked out of the charity gala, Emma quickly slipped into her chosen persona, tilting her head slightly and pasting on a vapid smile. "I'm sorry, sir. I was just heading for the little girls' room."

She used the breathy voice she'd practiced earlier with Amanda, since her usual no-nonsense voice wasn't "right" for her role.

She tried to step around him, but he shifted with her, blocking her escape.

Blinking in surprise, she looked up at him again. "You're...um...blocking my way, sir."

He didn't speak. Instead, he frowned thoughtfully down at her, one dark eyebrow lifting in question.

"You...aren't going to stop a lady from..." she faked a stupid giggle and waved her fingers in the air as if that made complete sense to both of them. "You know."

He rolled his eyes, then took her upper arm, leading her forcibly towards the patio doors. "What...?" She tried to pull away, but he didn't release her arm. "What are you doing?"

"We're going to have a private talk," he murmured, leaning in to growl the words into her ear.

Emma ignored the shiver of...something strange...at the sound of his sexy voice.

"And if I don't want to have a private talk?" she demanded, still trying to reclaim her arm. Her breathy voice vanished, replaced by her normal tone. Being dragged about by a stranger definitely wasn't the time to play the coquette.

"Tough," was his only reply.

By this point, they were already through the door and Emma tried one more time to jerk her arm free. This time he released her and she stepped away, looking around at the dimly lit terrace. "What do you want?"

He shook his head, crossing his arms over his chest. "Aren't you supposed to be playing the vapid bimbo?"

Emma glared daggers up at him. "Why do you care?"

He shrugged, dropping his arms and tucking his hands into the pockets of his dark slacks. "Curiosity mostly. I want to know why."

Emma shifted her purse to under her other arm and deposited her glass of champagne on the edge of the stone balustrade. She wanted her hands free, just in case she needed to defend herself. She wasn't getting the "I'm going to hurt you" vibe, but obviously, she must be a bit muddled if she'd allowed herself to be dragged out onto the stupid terrace!

Or maybe she was distracted by the pain inflicted by these awful shoes!

Pulling herself together, she tilted her head slightly to the side and gave him her pretend smile. "Why what?" she asked, feigning confusion. "I'm here to party. Just like everyone else." Thankfully, there were other guests on the terrace, and they seemed to be enjoying the festivities.

She lifted her hand and twirled a lock of hair coyly around her finger, hoping that she was doing it correctly.

"Stop it," the man growled. "You're not a dimwit," he sliced one hand through the air. "Just knock off the act!"

Emma rolled her eyes, dropping the lock of hair. Giving up the pretense, she allowed her anger to surface. "Look!" she snapped, poking the giant in the middle of his chest with her finger, "You're right, I'm *not* an air-head. But I'm here to do a job. And right now, you are getting in my way. So if you don't want to help me, then get out of my way!"

With that, she grabbed a handful of her annoying dress to lift the hem and turned to leave. Unfortunately, he wasn't finished with her. He grabbed her arm again, nearly making her stumble in the process. "What's your endgame?"

Emma was not going to take his he-man antics any longer. She considered calling for help, but the look in his eyes dared her to try it. Irritated by his arrogance, she fought to control her temper. "You think you're beyond challenging, don't you?"

Even in the dim light, Emma could see the spark of amusement in the man's dark eyes. "Something like that," he replied. "Spill it!" He leaned closer. "What's your game?"

Emma crossed her arms over her chest and glared up at him. Unfortunately, the effect was ruined when her silk purse hit the floor with a loud thud.

"Darn it!" she muttered and started to bend down to grab it. But he was faster and plucked the red clutch up and, without even a hint of remorse for violating the sanctity of a woman's purse, opened it and peered inside. When his long, tanned fingers plucked her cell phone out of the interior, his thumb moving over the screen to unlock it, she wasn't sure what his expression revealed. Her stomach warned her that it wasn't good.

Sure enough, he saw Amanda's text message, *"No! Avoid that guy!*

He's Prince Rayed el Mitra of Fahre! Avoid! Alert Alert! Warning – stay away! He won't work!"

It seemed as if he was holding onto his anger by a thin, tenuous thread. "Why won't I work?" he demanded through clenched teeth. "What plan are you and your friend..." he paused to check the message again, reading the name, "...Amanda trying to pull? Are you going to trap some poor schmuck into marriage? Or are you scamming one of the guests here tonight?"

Marriage? Good grief! Hell no! And scamming someone? Oh boy, did this guy have it all wrong! "No!" Emma hissed, trying to grab her phone. But he lifted the phone out of her reach, smirking down at her.

His jaw clenched tightly and he leaned closer. "Explain it to me then!" he growled. "And if there's *anything* illegal going on, I'm calling the police!"

Emma's jaw dropped, but she caught herself quickly. For several precious seconds, she considered how to answer. In the end, she suspected he could be an asset, even if Amanda disagreed.

With a huff, she turned slightly, checking for eavesdroppers on the terrace even as she lowered her voice. The cool night air tended to carry sounds more easily. "I suspect that there's something illegal happening, but I don't know what it is! There have been some odd headlines by some potentially unsavory politicians lately that don't make sense. The people involved in those headlines are here tonight, and will be in Philadelphia for the next several days. I want to find out if there is more to the headlines than what they appear to be." She shifted on her feet, thinking about burning the shoes when she got back to the apartment tonight. "Unfortunately, I haven't figured out what's actually happening," she explained. "Yet!" She poked his chest again. "And if you start spreading that information around, then I will flip the switch and play the ditzy girl again, which will make you look like a fool!"

The giant man stared at her for a stunned moment, then threw his head back, laughing at her explanation. The man actually laughed! Emma watched in fascination as he laughed with all of his body, enjoying whatever joke he thought she'd just told him.

The ridiculous thought that the guy had a sexy neck popped into her head, but she hurriedly banished it. There was no such thing as a sexy neck!

His laugh was pretty nice though.

The man's laughter faded, but the amusement lingered in his dark eyes as he said, "Honey, you couldn't look ditzy even when trying. I saw through the "stupid" routine instantly."

That was an interesting point and she tilted her head, curiosity rising despite her increasing ire. "How? What did I do wrong?" She actually stepped closer. "Can you explain what I did wrong? Because...well, I'm just...I need to figure some things out. Those issues could be vitally important and you're right, I'm struggling to play a ditz properly."

He reached out, tapping her along her temple with a finger. "It's here," he said, his voice softening to a rough, husky growl. "I can see the intelligence in your eyes, *eazizi*." That finger made a slow, taunting path down the side of her face. "The red dress was a good effort, but your sharp, intelligent gaze was a dead giveaway."

Even as he spoke, his eyes moved down over her figure in the red dress. She trembled and her breasts...they seemed to swell under the weight of his gaze. Her nipples tightened and Emma was terrified that the thin silk material revealed exactly what she was feeling. Her fears were confirmed when she saw his triumphant half-smile. "Point made," he purred, his voice even lower.

Had he moved closer? Why were their faces mere inches apart? Was he about to kiss her? She should stop him. Emma knew she should tell him to go to hell. She could find another event and another guy. Or maybe she'd figure out a new plan over the next few days. She'd get into these events somehow, she vowed.

And yet, Emma couldn't seem to move away. She forgot to breathe for a moment as she lost herself in his dark gaze.

"Are you going to turn me in?" she whispered, her heart pounding, but not out of fear. Well, yes, out of fear. But the fear was caused by this intense awareness of the man versus the other kind of fear. The fear born out of the risk of being caught at an event to which she hadn't been invited.

His eyes sharpened, but the laughter lingered on his upturned mouth. "Are you going to be honest with me?"

Honest? She shrugged, proud of herself for not snorting at the man's question. "Probably not."

He laughed, pushing away from the wall on which he'd been leaning. "Fair enough. If you're not going to be honest and tell me the details of what's going on, then I'm just going to have to keep you by my side for the evening."

And with that, he took her hand and tugged her back inside, barely pausing to give her time to gather the dress so she didn't trip on the hem again.

"Where are we going?" she demanded, feeling as if her toes were about to fall off as she hurried to keep up with him in her impossibly high heels.

"To dance," he told her. He also noticed that she was struggling to keep up with his longer stride and slowed down, for which she was intensely grateful.

She huffed a bit, but her indignation was fake. "What if I don't know how to dance?"

He didn't even shrug as he continued towards the dance floor. "Then I will guide you through the steps," he explained as if it was obvious.

Before she realized where they were, he spun her into his arms. Because of her dress and the dangerously long hem, she was off balance and fell against his chest. But strong hands held her, pulling her in close and keeping her steady.

Emma stared up at him, startled by the amount of heat emanating from him. He was like a furnace! She figured out why when she put her hand on his shoulder. There were muscles underneath the wool of his tuxedo jacket. Lots of muscles! No padding, she realized and her fingers slid along the material, examining and exploring. Her eyes dropped to his chest and she mentally stripped him of his clothes. As soon as she realized what she was doing, she gasped in dismay and aimed her wandering eyes firmly at his Adam's apple.

The soft, husky laughter warned her that her visual exploration hadn't gone unnoticed.

Knowing she was caught, both literally and figuratively, she groaned with irritation. "Shut up!" she snapped and looked away. His only response was to pull her closer, his strong arms wrapping around her. She felt the soft, husky laugh as it vibrated through his chest, trying to suppress the shiver of...of what? She wasn't pleased that she'd made him laugh. The oaf was laughing *at her*!

But, for some reason, his hold on her didn't feel threatening. It was... somehow both comforting and exciting. His hand splayed over her back, singeing the skin with his heat. And yet, she also felt safe and secure in his arms. He was like a giant grizzly bear. One that she'd like to snuggle up against, completely unconcerned by his claws and teeth.

Okay, that was a lie! She was terrified of his teeth. But not at the moment. The man had big teeth, after all! And grizzly bears were grumbly and grouchy.

Sighing, she leaned against him, enjoying the moment until she realized what she was doing and pulled away.

"Stop it," he grumbled and pulled her closer again, easily steering them through the steps to dance along with the music.

She enjoyed the dance, letting herself fall into step with him. For this moment, she allowed herself to simply be. To enjoy and to appreciate that a man of his size was graceful enough to dance. And she doubted he looked silly doing it.

As the music soothed and his big, strong body teased hers, awakening thoughts and desires she'd thought long gone, Emma wondered what she was doing. This wasn't supposed to be a night of pleasure. She was here to work. She had a mission!

"You're tensing on me again," he warned, his lips brushing the sensitive shell of her ear.

Shocked at the touch, as well as at the intense desire that shot through her, Emma pulled back, looking up at him with confusion and…and several other strange, unfamiliar emotions. "You're dangerous."

He nodded. "More than you can ever know."

"I should go."

"You should stay here."

She laughed, rolling her eyes even as he twirled her around, his strong arms lifting her slightly so she didn't trip on the hem of her dress.

"Tell me more about why you're here."

Heart thudding, she shrugged one shoulder delicately, as if his question, and his touch, wasn't causing her to tremble. Why did he have to be so…so aware! So intelligent that he could see through her so easily! "Why are you here?"

He grinned, a devilish expression if ever she'd seen one. "I'm avoiding something at home."

She tilted her head slightly. "You don't seem like the kind of man to be afraid of anything."

He emitted a low growl at her words. "I didn't say that I was afraid. I just said I was avoiding a situation in which I am not comfortable."

She felt her hair cascade over her shoulders as she tilted her head back, looking into his dark, mesmerizing eyes. "Isn't that the same as running away?"

"No."

Emma laughed, oddly charmed by his gruff replies. "I bet you growl instead of snore at night, don't you?"

He lifted that dark eyebrow, silently demanding that she explain her comment.

"Never mind," she sighed. "I really do need to leave. You've ruined my plan for the evening. I'm going to have to come up with a new one."

His hold around her waist didn't loosen. "Tell me your old plan. Maybe I can help."

She grinned and started to pull out of his arms. The music had changed to a faster song and she wasn't sure she could handle the increased pace along with the slightly dragging hem of her dress. "I'm leaving now."

The man recaptured her hand, holding her from walking away from him. "How did you get here?"

"Doesn't matter."

"It matters to me," he argued, taking her hand and tucking it onto his elbow as he led her towards the exit. "I'll see you home."

"What if I drove here?"

"Then I'll ensure that you are delivered safely to your vehicle." He paused, looking down at her. "But I bet you took a cab, didn't you?'

"Yes," she grimaced, frustrated that he was able to read her so easily. "Seriously, stop being so intuitive!"

He laughed again and Emma decided that she enjoyed the sound.

Rayed patted her hand where it rested on his arm. "You're an interesting woman to observe."

She laughed at that and he pulled her against his side. She leaned into him as she said, "You're probably an arrogant bastard and I shouldn't let you lead me around like this."

He kissed the top of her head. "I'm a very arrogant bastard. But you like me anyway."

She snorted, causing several of the guests to turn and gape at her. Emma wondered about that for a moment, but by the time she realized why, they were already outside in the crisp night air.

"Wait a minute!" she gasped and pulled out of his arms. She stepped back, glaring up at him angrily. "You're a freaking prince!" she said in an accusatory voice.

His eyes instantly shuttered and he watched her with a blank expression now. "I am. Is that a problem?"

She tilted her head to the side and surveyed him. "Are you one of those rich jerks who think they can use and abuse women for sport and his own warped amusement?"

He lifted a dark eyebrow again.

She glared at the offending eyebrow and pointed up to it as she warned, "You know, I could shave that off."

He blinked at her, not sure what she meant. Emma lifted a hand and tapped her own eyebrow. Her statement only caused him to stare at her for another long moment, then he threw back his head, laughing at her again. While still chuckling, he reached out and took her hand. "Come along, *aleaziz*."

She let him enclose her fingers in his big hand, shocked by the jolt of electricity. "You don't have to drag me around, you know. You could be a gentleman and just..." He paused as a big, sleek limousine pulled up beside the curb. Several men in dark suits with ear pieces jumped out, opening the door and speaking in a foreign language.

"Wait a minute!" she gasped.

"What's wrong now?" he asked, looking down at her as he placed her hand onto his arm. She pulled that hand away and grabbed her phone, snapping pictures at him, then sent the message to Amanda. When she slipped her phone back into the small clutch, she smiled triumphantly up at him. "There. If I wind up dead in an alley or dumped into the river, then my roommate can send the pictures to the police."

He stared at her for a long moment, then rolled his eyes. Impatiently, he gestured to the interior of the limousine. "Get in the..." he stopped and looked down at her, a stunned expression in his darkly handsome features. "Wait...what's your name?"

She smiled, unaware of her dimples coming out. "I'm Emma Gianni."

He moved closer, towering over her now. "And what do you do, Ms. Gianni?"

Her smile faded away at his closeness. At this distance, which was nothing at all, she could smell him. Not just his aftershave, but the scent of him. The maleness of him. He was...delicious! He was all man and musk and some indefinable scent that caused her nostrils to flare with heat, desire coiling inside of her. "Don't kiss me," she whispered.

His expression barely altered, but he replied, "I'm going to kiss you, Emma." One dark eyebrow lifted, as if daring her to challenge him.

She wanted to shake her head. She was usually the one in charge during any sort of romantic interlude. She made the rules in the relationship. She was the one who kissed the men, who decided on the dates, paid for the meals and entertainment, and called the shots. She decided when and where, how and how much, she always strictly controlled the men she allowed into her life.

She could tell this man would never allow himself to be controlled. "I don't have time for you," she whispered, something inside of her rebelling at the idea of never seeing him again.

She felt his fingers clench on her waist. When had he put his hands on her waist?

"You will *make* time for me, Emma."

Her breath hitched and she glared up at him. "You haven't even told me your name."

"You know my name." His finger lifted, trailing a path of fire down her cheek. "Say my name, Emma."

"No," she whispered. Saying his name would be too...too...intimate!

"Why not?"

She closed her eyes, breathing in his scent. Leaning closer, she inhaled, wanting to memorize the scent, to savor it and save it for later. "Because saying your name is too..." she opened her eyes, looking up at him. She didn't finish, afraid of what she might reveal if she finished.

"Too intimate," he finished for her, nodding knowingly. He wrapped a hand around the back of her neck and started to pull her closer. Fortunately, something stopped him and he sighed, pressing his forehead to hers. "Get in the limo, Emma. I'm not going to make love to you right here in the parking lot."

His words, spoken so softly, but with a rough, lilting accent, soothed and surprised her. She tossed them around in her mind, treasuring them and smiling because his words meant that he felt it too.

Then she realized what he'd just said and she pulled back, startling them both. "No!"

He chuckled. "You like that word too much, Emma."

She laughed along with hm, but still shook her head. "I can't get into that limousine..." she paused and tilted her head again. "What's the appropriate way to address you?'

"My name is Rayed."

"Rayed," she repeated, tossing his name around in her head, enjoying the experience of the word in her mind. "That sounds so exotic."

He shook his head, maintaining eye contact. "It's an ordinary name in my country."

Her smile widened. "Emma is an ordinary name here in the United States," she admitted. "We're a well-matched pair."

He laughed, then stepped back. "Get in the limo, Emma. I promise that you will arrive at your destination safely and un-kissed."

She bit her lip, contemplating his promise. She hadn't consciously realized what she was doing until he growled and stepped towards her. With a yelp, she backed up, then in a daring move that she might regret later, Emma dove into the limo, sliding all the way to the far side as if distance could help protect her.

It didn't. She realized that as soon as he entered, even if he kept to the opposite side of the limousine.

She noticed that someone closed the door, then watched as several men jogged around the limousine. "Who are those men?"

"My body guards."

Her eyes widened. " You need body guards?" she asked, leaning forward curiously. The limousine started moving at that point and she fell back against the soft leather, but continued to watch Rayed. "Are you in danger?"

He shrugged dismissively, as if the threat of danger wasn't worth worrying about. "Nothing out of the ordinary."

Emma didn't understand what that was supposed to mean, but since he reached out, covering her hand where it lay on the soft leather of the seat, she was too stunned by the heat emanating from his hand to hers to think about it. A moment later, she pulled her eyes away from the intensity of his gaze, blinking at the darkened space.

Before she could speak, the limousine moved forward. "I'm not going to die, am I?" she asked, flipping around so that she was sitting on the opposite side of the large seat that directly faced him.

He chuckled and, for some odd reason, the sound was reassuring. "I guarantee that you will arrive at your home safely and in one piece. I don't have any..." he stopped himself.

"You were going to say that you don't have any ill-intentions, weren't you." It wasn't a question. Emma smirked at his chagrinned expression.

He tilted his head slightly, acknowledging the accuracy of her question. "Correct."

Emma shifted on the seat, still glaring, but she folded her hands over her crossed legs, her foot wiggling in the air the only clue that she was nervous. "But you couldn't finish the statement because you *do* have ill-intentions."

One corner of his mouth quirked upwards. "That's also correct," he replied, his long legs stretching out in front of him, his feet precariously close to hers.

"Perhaps not of the machete-and-dismembered-body-parts kind of intentions though?" she offered hopefully.

The man laughed, a large, robust sound that sent shivers of awareness throughout her body and did some sort of melty thing to her stomach. It was a nice, if dangerous, sound.

When his amusement faded, he looked at her, devilment shimmering in his dark eyes. "No, dismemberment never passed through my mind."

Emma nodded, her toes curling at his sexy, mesmerizing smile. But she was still trying to feign casual sophistication. "Good to know," she said with a nod. She stared back at him, the silence heavy as velvet between them. She could feel her heart thudding, her body throbbing with awareness. Her heartrate sped up as his eyes lowered, his gaze moving over her body.

"Stop it," she whispered, feeling every muscle react to his visual caress. His eyes lifted and she felt her breathing speed up.

"Stop what?" he asked, his voice a silken stroke of grizzly-bear roughness.

"Stop doing that." Emma knew that she wasn't making a lot of sense. And yet, his lips curling upwards indicated that he knew what "that" was. Even more crazy, she knew that he wasn't going to stop.

The limousine came to a smooth stop and Emma looked through the windows. Why was she disappointed that they'd arrived at her apartment complex? "We're here."

Emma sighed. For some silly reason, her heart sank. The ride was over? Their interlude was finished?

"I'll walk you to your door," he announced, then stepped out of the door that had magically opened.

Emma stared, aware of several issues. The first of which was how he... or his driver...had known where she lived. Because she was a journalist, one that often delved into the criminal underworld, she was careful to keep her address off of the internet. So, how in the world had he found her address?

Emma didn't have time to figure that problem out because Rayed extended hand, patiently waiting for her to take it, to slide her fingers into the large, tanned hand. She knew that his touch would banish everything except that tingling awareness.

Refusing to be a coward, Emma reached out and took his hand, swallowing a gasp as his fingers tightened around hers. He held her hand while she exited, bowing low so that she didn't knock her head. When she straightened up, he was right there. So close! And breathtakingly handsome as he stared down at her.

"Thank you," she whispered, thinking she should pull her hand away. But her fingers felt too good right there in his hand.

"You're welcome." For another long moment, they stood there in the apartment complex parking lot. Emma felt as if she couldn't take a deep breath and she didn't care! All she wanted was for this man to pull her into his arms so she could experience those same amazing sensations she'd felt during their dance earlier in the evening.

He moved closer. "Emma, which is your apartment?"

"Why?" she asked, then groaned, her free hand lifting to rub her forehead. "Stupid question." She looked around, then pointed vaguely to the second story of the garden style apartments. "I'm up there."

Rayed nodded, then tucked her hand onto his arm as he led her towards the stairway. "This is a nice area," he commented, looking around as his other hand patted hers.

"It's convenient," she replied, not understanding his interest in the generic apartment complex. It was nice enough, but there wasn't anything extraordinary about the place. There were about ten buildings scattered around the property, all with two stories. Each building probably had about eight apartments? Emma wasn't sure since the number of dwellings hadn't been something she'd cared about.

He moved and his big, muscular body brushed against hers. All thoughts about the property slipped out of her mind, replaced by the scent of this man and how extraordinarily enticing he was.

"In what way?" he asked.

What in the world was he talking about? Emma looked around at the darkened apartment complex in confusion.

Right! The property! She'd rather discuss his scent. Although, perhaps it was rude to ask the man for the name of his aftershave. She'd love to get some so she could put some on her pillow every night!

He looked at her curiously and she struggled to remember what he'd asked her. Property! Darn it!

Emma shrugged as they continued walking across the silent parking lot. "It's not all that interesting, the apartments. I live with my best friend and the rent is reasonable. Plus, the highway is conveniently close. Otherwise, it's just an unremarkable apartment."

"It is interesting because you live here, Emma," he told her.

Emma frowned thoughtfully. She looked up at him, wondering if that was just a smooth line. The guy knew all the right things to say, but that only made her more wary.

They were standing outside of her apartment door now. "Thank you for the ride home." She smiled weakly as she lifted her eyes to stare at his chin. "You saved me about twenty dollars. That's a whole bottle of wine in my world." She looked out at the parking lot where the limousine as well as two black, scary looking SUVs waited for him. "I guess that's not much in your world." She looked back up at him. "But it is in mine."

Before she could say another word, Rayed lifted her hand to his lips and pressed a kiss to her knuckles before nibbling on her fingertips. The sensation was so erotic, she couldn't stop the gasp of surprise.

"It was my pleasure, Emma," he replied, then placed her hand on his shoulder. "And now I'm going to kiss you." He moved closer, his hands resting heavily on her hips as he pulled her against him. "Any objections?"

She should object. She should step away from Rayed because he was going to hurt her. Not in a physical sense. She wasn't sure how she knew that, but her instincts told her that he would never hurt a woman. But he was going to hurt her tender, cautious heart. She'd never been in love before, but Rayed was the kind that...!

He kissed her. When his mouth covered hers, the world seemed to spin. His lips were warm and surprisingly soft against hers and she moaned. Yes, this was what she'd wanted. Emma felt as if she'd been waiting for this kiss all her life!

Leaning into him, she reached up, her fingers diving into his surprisingly soft, thick hair, deepening the kiss. She didn't want the soft, teasing kisses. She wanted...yes!

As soon as he felt her fingers in his hair, Rayed was lost. Her touch left a trail of shimmers along his skin and the desire he'd been barely controlling since he'd first set eyes on her, burst into an all-consuming wildfire of need.

His fingers tangled in her long, silky hair as he angled her head slightly so he could deepen the kiss, while his other arm tightened around her waist, pulling her closer, craving the feeling of her softness against his body. Needing to consume her, to devour her!

He'd never felt desire like this before. It raged through his very bones, leaving him unaware of the world. When her tongue met his, he groaned. Or had she made that sound?

He wanted to lift her up and fill her with his hardness right here in the dark hallway. He wanted to rip that red gown off and see what his hands could only feel. He wanted to make her feel as crazed as he did at this moment. And he wanted to feel her hands all over his body.

He was just about to suggest that they move somewhere more private, when the apartment door was jerked open, jolting them back to reality.

He looked at the furious woman glaring up at him, then down at Emma. With intense satisfaction, he realized that she was just as flummoxed as he was. Should he pull the door closed again? Order this strange woman with wild hair piled on top of her head and a threadbare tee shirt to go away?

"Inside!" the stranger snapped. Then, because Emma didn't move fast enough, she reached out and grabbed Emma's hand from his shoulder, pulling her away from him.

Emma didn't resist. He wanted to growl with frustration, but before he could react, Emma was jerked into the apartment. The strange woman gave him one more vicious glare and slammed the door in his face.

Well, that had been...unexpected, Rayed thought, bracing his hands on either side of the door jam in an effort to get his body back under control before he turned around and faced his guards. They wouldn't dare laugh at him, but his aroused state would be obvious if he walked away right now.

Breathing in slowly and letting the air flow out of his lungs in a whoosh, he slowly got his body back under control. The strange woman was probably the "Amanda" who had texted a warning to Emma about him earlier in the evening. Roommate? Or sister?

Most likely a roommate because the two women didn't look anything alike. Amanda had frizzy golden blond tresses while his Emma had dark, cascading hair that still made his hands itch to feel it sliding through his fingers. It wasn't very smooth anymore, he thought with satisfaction as he turned and faced his body guards, who were standing at a discreet distance and, thankfully, all looking away at the moment.

"Let's go," he snapped out and the guards turned, heading back down the stairs in their usual formation around him.

Something occurred to him as he stepped into the limousine, glancing once more up at the apartment where the lights were shimmering into the darkness; Emma hadn't realized that his guards had surrounded them. She'd been completely focused on him!

That was good. No, he corrected as the driver accelerated out of the parking lot, that was excellent! It proved that he wasn't the only one affected. Furthermore, he'd been on the verge of lifting Emma up and having sex with her against the damn wall of her apartment complex and damn the consequences. He hadn't even considered the consequences when she'd been in his arms! And he knew without a doubt that Emma wouldn't have stopped him if he'd...!

Rayed's body began throbbing again with painful arousal and he sighed, rubbing the bridge of his nose. Emma. Even her name was pretty and sweet.

"What the hell is wrong with you?" Alfred Monterey demanded, watching as his underlings shoved Governor Kevin Mitchell into his study.

Governor Mitchell, "Mitch" to his voters and friends, glared at the man who had just manhandled him. How dare someone put their hands on him! He was the freaking governor of a very influential state and this person...was nothing more than a mere employee of some two-bit internet service provider!

As the goons exited the room, Kevin jerked his jacket back into place. "Who the hell do you think you are?" Kevin snapped, pulling himself up to his full height of five feet, seven inches. Yeah, he was on the short side, but he had power. And no underling was going to push him around!

Alfred muttered several epithets under his breath, watching the stupid politician. After a tense moment, Alfred shook his head and stepped over to the bar, pouring a large glass of brandy. He didn't bother to pour anything for the governor. He was a fool and it was better to not encourage his stupidity.

Turning away from the bar, he glared at Kevin. "The bitch in the red dress that you were drooling over tonight?" he began.

Kevin toyed with his lapel. "What woman?"

Alfred rubbed his forehead and dropped into one of the leather chairs. He took a sip of his brandy, not bothering to offer the other man a seat.

He'd forgotten that the governor was gay, so obviously, the man didn't notice hot women in gorgeous red dresses! True, the governor had a wife and four kids. But the wife was just a front. A political marriage. How the wife had gotten pregnant four times was a bit of a mystery, but also, none of Alfred's business. If the man needed to have a heterosexual disguise to ease the minds of his voters, so be it.

Alfred waved his glass of brandy in the general direction of the hotel they'd just left. "There was a gorgeous woman that crashed the party tonight. She took pictures of you with the various council members!" Alfred hissed. Leaning forward, he glared at the other man. "I told you to be careful and not allow yourself to be photographed at the event tonight!"

Kevin snorted and sat down, ignoring the insult of not being offered a brandy. "If some idiot was taking pictures of me with...!" He stopped suddenly and thought back about the evening. "If you saw some bitch in red, then get your...!" He stopped again, his heart pounding at the possibility that someone might have gotten pictures of him with the minions he'd ordered to vote for the candidates he was going to put forward for consideration.

Standing up, he started pacing nervously. But after several moments, Kevin stopped and shook his head. "No, I don't remember seeing anyone at the party tonight who could be an obstacle to our plans," he finished lamely. Kevin knew that his threats and illegal manipulations, what he politely termed "convincing" when anyone dared to ask him about his arm-twisting, had to happen at these social events. His blackmailing looked more casual when it was done in a social setting. Speaking with the council members in the governor's office would be logged and recorded, his conversations and meetings considered "official state business". That was why he'd been to the party tonight. Every conversation he had now regarding the internet deal had to be completely off the record.

Alfred sneered at Kevin, banishing some of Kevin's panic and replacing it with resentment.

"Do you remember seeing this woman tonight?" Alfred asked, flipping his cell phone around so that the governor could see the woman. She was stunningly beautiful and the red dress...it was hot! The woman had great curves! She wasn't one of those skinny bitches that looked like a well-dressed number two pencil. This beauty was soft and sweet in all the right places. And a stunner, to boot!

Kevin squinted at the image, then huffed. "How the hell am I supposed to know when someone is taking pictures of me? It happens all the time! I'm the freaking governor!" He walked over to the bar and pulled out the stopper to a bottle of bourbon. He poured a large amount into one of the crystal glasses, then slammed the drink back in one gulp and sighed as the heat burned down through his chest.

Alfred sighed impatiently and glared at the governor. "You have to be constantly aware of your surroundings! All the time! The only way that we're going to get away with this is if there's no connection between you and the people we're trying to pull in to help us push through the newest members of the board of directors! I thought you understood how this works!"

Kevin shrugged as he poured himself more bourbon. "Who cares about a few pictures of me chatting with some of the council members? I talk to dozens of people every day. As governor, it's my job to talk with the numerous council members that hold power in the various jurisdictions. It would be odd if I didn't talk to them."

Alfred rolled his eyes. "This woman has pictures of you, me, and two different council members from different towns. What's worse? She is a reporter! It might mean nothing now, but if anyone sees those pictures later, after the deal is announced and connects the dots, it's going to be a problem."

"A reporter?" Kevin blinked in alarm. "I thought Stella had assured us there wouldn't be any press at the events this week! How the hell had a reporter gotten in?"

Alfred deliberately ignored the governor's question. "It doesn't matter how she got in, Kevin," he snapped. "There will always be people taking pictures. She seemed to be a guest of some disgustingly wealthy prince. They left together and I saw them looking pretty intimate." He rubbed his forehead. "The point is, the pictures might be incriminating."

The governor's eyes narrowed, the implications of the woman's presence becoming clearer now. "So what the hell are you going to do about it?"

Alfred wanted to break his nose, but doubted he'd live to brag about it. "I'm going to handle it," he told the rather drunk governor. "But if our agreement is going to work, you need to be more careful!"

Kevin slammed back the rest of the bourbon and smacked the crystal goblet onto the table beside him. "Fine. But fix this issue and leave me out of it!" He stood up unsteadily and headed for the door. "Let me know when you need the next diversion." He chuckled and shook his head. "My assistant has some amazingly stupid headlines queued up. I love that prisoner idea from yesterday. It completely distracted and kept all the reporters jabbering on about the sterilization issue. It was a perfect way to keep those assholes occupied. Keeping them salivating over my crazy headlines means that they're not looking for the truth about what's coming up." And then he was gone.

Chapter 3

"Dragons." Emma rolled over in bed, staring at the ceiling as she thought back to her dream. It had been so vivid! In the dream, a vicious dragon with a scar on his face loomed over her. She'd known it had been a dream but Emma kept trying to scream. Unfortunately, she couldn't make a sound. The dragon hadn't done anything to her, but she couldn't shake the feeling that the scarred dragon was dangerous. "Very odd." She rarely had bad dreams, but last night's dream definitely qualified as a nightmare.

Turning her head, she tried to see what time it was. But her phone was...gone? Emma always left her phone on her bedside table, just in case her boss called during the night. Nighttime news stories were rare, but because they'd happened several times in the past, she was careful to ensure that her phone was easily accessible.

Rolling over, she looked around. It wasn't tangled in her sheets. Nor was it under her pillow. She got out of bed and checked the floor, relief surging through her when she found it on the floor right beside her bedside table instead of on the charging stand where she'd thought she had left it last night. She always put her phone on the charging stand before she fell asleep. It wasn't just the possibility of her boss calling her. If she woke up during the night, Emma needed to know what time it was. It was a weird quirk, but she couldn't get back to sleep until she knew the time.

How had her phone fallen? Had she knocked it off during her nightmare? Picking it up, she blinked until her eyes focused enough that she could read the time. Only six-thirty in the morning, which was good. Unfortunately, her phone was only at twenty percent battery power! Definitely not good! She never left home without a fully charged phone!

Pushing her hair out of her eyes, she sat back down on the bed. "Last night was definitely weird," she whispered to herself as she carefully set the phone on the charger and eyed her bed. The bedding didn't look abnormally mussed. Had she simply flailed her arm and knocked the phone off the charging platform?

She glanced at the door to her bedroom, but decided to shower instead of getting coffee first, which was her normal routine. Last night, Amanda had pulled her into the apartment, directly out of the arms of Rayed, and slammed the door. "We'll talk about this in the morning," she'd warned Emma. Normally, Amanda wasn't the "mom" figure in their friendship. But Emma had to agree that kissing Rayed last night hadn't been a wise decision.

She was due the lecture Amanda was sure to give her this morning. Hence, a shower before coffee seemed a better option. Whatever Amanda was going to say, and every sharp word would be justified, would be better absorbed after a shower and a big cup of coffee.

Twenty minutes later, Emma stepped out of her shower and found a steaming mug of coffee waiting on the counter. "Bless you!" Emma whispered to the steamy bathroom. Amanda had delivered the coffee at some point during Emma's shower. Nice!

She took a deep sip of the steaming brew, then padded barefoot into her bedroom. Dressing in a clean pair of jeans and a tee shirt, she threw on a sweater and ventured out into the family room, ready to face the expected lecture.

"What did you find out last night?" Amanda asked as soon as she saw Emma. Amanda was a mystery writer and a good one! She was currently working on her fourth mystery. Because she worked from home, Emma bounced news story ideas off of her friend. Amanda often used Emma's real life news stories in her plots, although with tweaks and a great deal of poetic license.

Emma's cup was halfway to her mouth when Amanda asked that question. "That's it? No lecture about last night?"

"Why would I lecture you?" Amanda asked, tossing Emma a banana.

It took more concentration than Emma had this early in the morning to balance her coffee while catching the banana. It fell to the floor and Emma sighed as she bent to pick it up. "Aren't you going to tell me how I was wrong to kiss Rayed last night?"

Amanda's eyebrows lifted. She leaned against the countertop with raised eyebrows. "He's 'Rayed' now? You're on a first name basis with the Crown Prince of Fahre?" Amanda nodded behind her coffee cup. "That's an impressive night!" she went to the fridge and got out the small container of milk. "But since you had your tongue down his throat when I opened the door, I guess you have the right to call the man whatever you like."

Emma colored at the memory of that world-shattering kiss. Even now, she could still feel the sensations that had rocked her from the first moment Rayed had touched her. Then there'd been the way he'd kissed her! Emma shivered, her heart pounding as memories came rushing back. Surely that was illegal! His mouth...and his lips...! She licked her lips at the memory of how delicious he'd tasted. Oh, and Emma couldn't forget how much she'd enjoyed the way he'd touched her, holding her so firmly and yet, his touch made her feel precious and cherished. He held her in a way that made her think that he didn't want to let her go.

Sighing, Emma knew that she wanted to feel his touch again, wanted to kiss him and experience those intense sensations all over again. Her fingers tightened around the coffee mug, unaware of the steam rising up to tickle her nose.

"Earth to Emma! Come back!" She paused, then shook her head. "You're going to have to stop that."

Emma blinked, her hazy gaze finding Amanda in front of her with an angry expression in her lovely, emerald eyes. "Stop what?" Emma asked, her cheeks warming again, but for a completely different reason this time.

Amanda tapped the tip of Emma's nose. "You're fantasizing about him again, aren't you?"

Emma choked on a laugh, but smothered her amusement at the irritation in her friend's eyes.

Shrugging slightly as she tried to dissipate the impact of those memories, she started to peel the banana. "He's a very nice man," she pointed out.

Amanda snorted. "He didn't look all that nice last night. He looked pretty darn naughty, in fact."

Emma stared at the now-peeled banana, her mind flashing back to the feel of...oh, his erection pressed against her stomach last night. Yes, that had been...impressive! Rayed was naughty? Yeah, very naughty. That was the perfect description for the way Rayed had kissed her. Naughty and delicious!

"Good grief!" Amanda snorted, turning around and stalking to her desk while shaking her head with disgust. "You're useless this morning." Amanda grabbed her cup and headed back into the kitchen, rinsed out her coffee cup and put it in the drying rack. "I have to meet with my publisher this morning." Amanda disappeared into her own room and, a second after that, the shower turned on.

Emma's smile disappeared and she stared down at her coffee. Amanda was right. Emma needed to get a grip on herself and figure out what was going on with yesterday's headlines. The headlines were too... off. The sensational headline about forcing prisoners to go through a life-altering surgery were just...wrong. Something was going on and Emma's plan to find a way to get into more of the events attended by the rich and powerful hadn't panned out last night. She'd been too overwhelmed by Rayed's presence last night to cozy up to any of the governors in attendance last night.

However, she'd failed miserably at her task.

That meant that Emma needed a new plan. Plan B could be something as simple as...?

Maybe she could...?

Sighing, Emma slouched down onto the couch, taking a bite of the banana. She didn't have a plan B. Emma was stumped.

Groaning, Emma stood back up, banana in one hand and coffee in the other as she went to her computer and sent off a message to her boss, letting her know what was going on with her assignment. Unfortunately, the sum total of the message was "not much".

Before Emma could start on a new message, the doorbell rang.

Amanda stepped out of her bedroom, dressed in a sleek pair of black slacks and a green sweater that perfectly matched her eyes.

"It's him, isn't it?" Amanda asked, opening her laptop. She made no move to answer the door. Instead, she started typing. "Are you going to get that?" she asked, her fingers flying over the keys even as she glanced at Emma. It was seriously impressive when Amanda did that. She was the only person Emma knew that could have a conversation with someone while typing in a completely different scene in her novel. It was wild!

Emma's cup froze halfway to her mouth and she blinked, not sure what to do. The doorbell rang again. Answer the door? For some reason, she didn't want to.

"Answer it," Amanda urged, still typing, but now she was staring at the monitor. "You and I both know it's him."

Still, Emma hesitated. "No, I actually have no idea who is on the other side of that door," Emma replied, then shifted on the sofa to start typing on her own laptop. She didn't have anything to write, but this was a game of chicken that Emma and Amanda played often. Neither of them wanted to answer the door, so both of them pretended to be too busy.

Unfortunately, in this instance, Amanda won. Mostly because Emma was too curious. It wasn't him, she told herself as she closed her laptop with a glare that Amanda ignored. Rayed wasn't behind the door.

Why would he be here? He was probably at some important meeting, discussing some crazy, billion-dollar investment. An investment that would earn him several more billions of dollars while Emma and Amanda rationed out the coffee grounds at the end of the month, unable to afford more until their next paycheck arrived.

Now, why did that sound as if she resented the man for making money? Maybe because she didn't have any at the moment. Grumbling, she yanked open the door, hoping to find a salesperson.

Instead, Rayed stood in the doorway, hands in his pockets, his jacket undone, and no tie. However, his suit was...gorgeous! The man must have a personal tailor because there just wasn't any way that a man could achieve that sophisticated a look with off the shelf clothing. Even the material looked too expensive for her to breathe on!

Emma stood there, clutching the door, feeling like all of the air had just left her body. He was just so...amazing! And tall! Had he been this tall last night? Yeah, probably. Men didn't grow several inches overnight.

Duh! She'd been wearing heels last night. While today...she glanced down at her bare feet. He did the same and her toes curled slightly as embarrassment washed over her. She hated standing in front of him, looking so dowdy when he was the epitome of sophistication.

"I'm outta here," Amanda grumbled, interrupting the tense moment. "One of you should speak though. Just a tip." Rayed stepped to the side so Amanda could leave.

Emma felt like calling out to her friend, demanding that she come back, to be here to protect her from the insane sensations that were already muddling her mind! But Amanda was gone. Goodness, her friend could move swiftly when she wanted to!

Finally, she turned back to Rayed. The man's dark eyebrow lifted and she felt her body heat up all over again.

Belatedly remembering her manners, she stepped aside, gesturing for him to enter.. "Would you like to come in?" she asked.

The corners of his lips quirked up slightly, but he bowed his head. "Yes. I would very much like to speak with you in private."

Did he have to duck to get through the doorway? Surely, that was just her imagination. He was tall, but he wasn't *that* tall, was he?

"How tall are you?" she blurted out, suddenly intensely curious.

He paused his perusal of her apartment, turning around to look down at her. "I'm six feet, four inches," he replied. "How tall are you? You seem shorter than you were last night." His eyes darted to her bare toes again. "I suppose you were wearing heels last night."

"Five feet, six," she answered. "And I was just thinking you seem taller this morning, so it must have been the shoes."

He nodded, not looking away from her. Were they really going to stand here, talking about shoes?

"Would you care to give me more details about what you were doing at the party last night?"

Ah! He was going to just dive right into it!

"No," she replied, enjoying the surprise in his eyes.

"No? You *aren't* going to tell me?"

She laughed, feeling slightly more relaxed now that she felt in control of the conversation. "Nope. It isn't any of your business why I was there."

He moved closer, the look in his eyes warning her that she wasn't in control. Not by a long shot! "Would you tell me if I guessed correctly?"

Emma doubted that the man could figure out her motives for being at such a dull event, but she shrugged, crossing her arms over her chest. "Sure. Why not? I've already told you some of it."

His smile widened. "If I guess correctly, do I get a kiss as a reward?"

Emma laughed again. "Sure. If you can figure out my reason for being at the charity ball last night, I'll give you a kiss." She felt fairly safe with that bet. How could he possibly know why she'd been at the event?

He pulled a hand out of his pocket and tapped a long, sexy forefinger against his nose as if considering the options. Finally, he said, "You've already told me that you were there trying to figure out if something illegal is going on. However, you didn't explain why you were playing the ditz. I suspect," he paused, examining her features, "that you were at the charity event last night so that you could find a man who could give you entrée into the exclusive parties, determined to play a ditz in order to put others off their guard so that you might hear things that they don't want you to hear. And," he continued, chuckling at her stunned expression, "you think that Governor Mitchell is the person doing the illegal activities because of the crazy headline about sterilization. You think that the headline was a way to pull attention away from whatever his real goal is."

Emma's mouth fell open! "How could you...?"

He threw back his head, laughing at her stunned expression. He lowered his head, kissing her softly, but with a sensuality that was shocking. He pulled back, leaving her lips tingling.

"I cheated," he admitted.

She blinked, not sure what he meant. "Cheated...how?" She looked around warily, wondering if he'd somehow installed listening devices in her apartment.

He shrugged, his hand sliding into his pants pockets again as he wandered around the family room. "I own a large share of stocks in your newspaper. I went to your editor and asked what you were working on. She gave me the details."

Emma's arms dropped to her sides and she glared at him. "That *is* cheating!"

He grinned. "Yes, I'd already admitted to that."

Her eyes narrowed again. "You don't look very repentant."

He chuckled. "Perhaps because I'm completely unrepentant." He moved over to her again. "Would it make things better if I told you that I could help?"

Help? How could he...? The devilish look in his dark eyes gave her the answer. "No!"

He shook his head at her reply, tsking her. "That's not a good attitude for an up and coming journalist, Emma." He leaned in. "I read your other articles last night. You're very good. I especially liked the piece on the homes by the ocean that are losing their yards because of the rising sea levels and the piece on the gorillas in the zoo. Doesn't seem fair about why the local teachers' unions are upset. Your presentations on the pros and cons of for-profit charter schools versus the public schools was excellent. I like how you explain both sides to the stories you publish, allowing the reader to agree or disagree with the proposed policies without trying to influence their opinion. The teacher's union story was particularly insightful."

His praise warmed her heart and she couldn't stop the mushy, happy feeling that welled up within her.

"Thank you," she whispered, lowering her lashes to hide her reaction. "I wish I could say that I looked you up last night, but my feet ached and..." she stopped, remembering how she'd lain in bed last night thinking about him, about his kiss, and wishing that he hadn't stopped.

"You missed me last night, didn't you?" he finished for her, his voice low and husky. Emma was just about to deny it, not wanting to give him that much power. But he stroked her cheek with a finger and she shivered. "I missed you too. I ached to have you in my bed."

Woah! She'd been thinking about a kiss! He'd just leaped over to... okay, she was a liar. She'd gone down the "making love" path too.

Clearing her throat, she looked around, trying to remember what they'd been discussing. "Right. Well, that's...!" What? What was it? "Nice," she finished lamely. "However, I really need to get some work done."

He shook his head slightly. "You need someone who can get you into the exclusive parties that are happening this week with all of the governors in town as well as the other politicians and wealthy donors," he corrected.

Darn it, he was right. She wasn't giving in though. She lifted her chin, folding her arms over her chest as she said, "Yes, but I can't do that with you."

"Why not?"

Rayed watched the myriad expressions flit across Emma's lovely face, utterly fascinated by her. He suspected that she was normally excellent at hiding her feelings. But he'd been reading experienced diplomats and world leaders all his life. His father had raised him and his older brother to understand the world and the various motivations of individuals. Hence, the lovely, adorable, enchanting Emma wasn't difficult to read.

"I can get you in," he told her, his voice low. He didn't want to scare her, but there was no way he would step aside and allow someone else to escort her around. He'd watched his brother and his new wife, Lila, for the past year. They were very much in love and, he suspected that he could have that same kind of relationship with Emma. The passion was there. And the fascination. Was there love? No. But for a man who hadn't even believed in love until he'd witnessed his older brother develop a relationship with a woman he'd been secretly infatuated with for more than a decade, an infatuation that had morphed into a deep love and respect on both sides, Rayed was more than willing to go after a woman that might give him the same sort of partnership.

"No!" she repeated firmly, even taking a step back in an effort to disburse the impact of his closeness on her libido. It was a pointless effort, she discovered. Distance didn't seem to help. She couldn't stop thinking about the kiss from last night. And wondering if she'd ever have the chance to experience it again.

"Why not?" he asked, appearing calm even as she felt the weight of his gaze drift over her body.

She crossed her arms again, glaring up at him. "Because of the kiss last night."

He chuckled. "I thought it was a pretty darn good kiss."

Emma shifted on her feet, her eyes fluttering downwards, then back up to glare at him. "It was *too* good," she admitted honestly.

Immediately, he shook his head. "There's no such thing as 'too good' when it comes to kissing." His amusement deepened. "As well as other...activities."

Emma felt that smile all the way down to her still-curled toes. Goodness, the man was potent! "You'll be a distraction. I have a job to do and if you're with me, then you'll distract me from my mission."

Rayed stared down at the woman, startled by her honesty. He was used to women playing coy. He was used to their lies and deceit. In his experience, women did whatever they could to get him into their beds. He had learned to constantly be on guard during sexual interludes. But Emma, with her bright, blue eyes and her gorgeous cascade of dark hair, enticed him like no other ever had. Then she had to go and stun him with her honesty!

Determinedly, he reached into the inside pocket of his jacket, noting that Emma tensed with the movement. He wasn't sure what that meant, but continued to watch her eyes as he slid the thick vellum out of his pocket. Waving the invitation at her, he watched her stubborn expression morph into curiosity.

"What's that?" She straightened up, her hands by her sides but he noticed her fingers wiggling with anticipation.

"An invitation to tonight's Bethmair Yacht Club party."

The wiggling in Emma's fingers expanded to encompass her whole body. She was literally vibrating with energy and excitement. Unexpectedly, she stepped forward and plucked the invitation from his hands.

"The Bethmair party!" She ran a careful finger over the embossed text. When those blue eyes lifted to his again, they were shimmering with eagerness and Rayed's body tightened with lust. "How did you...?" She stopped that question when he lifted an eyebrow. "Right. You've got that whole prince thing going for ya. You probably get invited to all the best parties."

"I do. Ya gotta love that 'prince thing', right?" Rayed teased. He stepped forward and plucked the invitation from her hand, sliding it back into his jacket, daring her to try and retrieve it. "I will pick you up at six o'clock tonight."

With that, he turned, walking out of the apartment and pulling the door firmly closed behind him before he scooped her up and carried her off to her bedroom to make love to her. Too soon, he told himself. Definitely too soon for sex. As fiery and passionate as their kiss had been, and Rayed had no doubt that if he'd continued kissing her, he could have had sex with her...regardless, he sensed that Emma wasn't casual about sex. A night with Emma would be significant.

He paused at the bottom step and realized that sex with Emma would be significant for him too. She was going to be his. Last night's kiss, as well as this morning's banter, light-hearted on the surface but with intense undercurrents of awareness on both sides, told him that Emma was the woman he'd been looking for. She was going to be his. Forever!

Stepping into the SUV, he tried to focus his mind on the next business meeting. However, the idea that he might have found his future wife meant that he could return home. Suddenly, a wave of longing for his desert country, the heat of the sunshine, and the endlessness of the deserts to the south of the capital city...he missed his home. He missed his family.

But he wouldn't go back until he had Emma on his arm. He couldn't face the happiness that Tazir and Lila shared until he'd found that happiness as well.

Chapter 4

"You look great!" Amanda whispered, admiring Emma as she twirled in the shimmering, peach cocktail dress. "And those heels won't be nearly as painful as the red ones you wore yesterday."

Emma groaned. "Those things should be banned!"

Her friend laughed, nodding her head. "I agree. I only wore them once and vowed to throw them out after that."

"Why didn't you?" Emma hissed, tucking her wallet, new peach lipstick, and keys into a small, black purse.

"Nostalgia," her roommate replied. Then added a small shrug as she continued, "And maybe a little bit of payback."

Emma froze, and then turned to frown at her friend. "Payback? For what?"

Amanda shrugged casually, twirling in her office chair. "Remember last month, when you left me alone at the table and the creepy guy we'd been ignoring from the bar showed up?"

Emma grimaced. "Yeah, sorry about that. I didn't realize he'd take my chair when I got up to use the restroom."

"Payback," her friend repeated smugly.

Emma stuck out her tongue at Amanda and mentally vowed never to leave her friend alone in public in the future. She'd wet her pants before leaving Amanda to the creepy creatures that lurked around a bar, waiting for a lone lady. Amanda's musical laughter was immediately followed by the doorbell.

"My chariot!" Emma sighed, smoothing her hand down over her stomach. The dress made her skin look warmer, but was it too short? The flirty skirt might fly up in the wind. Thankfully, it wasn't a terribly windy day today, so hopefully she'd be okay.

"Maybe I should change," she fretted, checking her image in the small mirror over the dresser that they used as a television stand. They'd found the gorgeous dress, as well as the red silk dress from the previous night, at the thrift store during one of their Saturday treks for coffee and bargains. But was this dress too much?

Amanda rolled her eyes. "Maybe you should stop procrastinating and answer the door."

Emma shifted on her feet. "Maybe you could answer it for me?"

Amanda chuckled. "Maybe you should pull up your big girl panties and answer the stupid door. You know he's gorgeous." Amanda chuckled as she stood up. "Besides, I need to stay out of range. Whenever you and that hottie are close by, the sparks flying around are dangerous to innocent bystanders."

Emma made a disgusted sound. "Since when were you ever innocent?"

Amanda didn't reply as she floated out of Emma's bedroom and hid in her own.

"I thought you were my friend!" Emma called out.

"I sure fooled you then, didn't I?" Amanda laughed through her bedroom door. "Answer the dang door!" she called when the bell chimed again.

Emma walked slowly to the door, nervously smoothing her hair. Was the dress too much? Or not enough?

"Emma," Rayed called out.

How did he know that she was on the other side of the door? That was really creepy! She yanked open the door and glared up at him. She wasn't as startled by his height as she'd been this morning. Probably because she was wearing three inch heels which gave her a slight height boost. But it wasn't enough, she thought with a nervous pang.

"You're still terrifying," she whispered in place of a greeting.

He laughed softly and stepped into the room, pressing her back against the wall just inside of the doorway. "And you're still stunningly beautiful!"

He kissed her then. Just a light kiss so she didn't have to worry about smudging her makeup. But it was enough to make her senses tingle again.

"Let's get out of here before we're unable to leave," he grumbled, taking her hand and pulling her out of the apartment.

Emma hurried after him, but on the precarious heels, it was difficult to balance and she jerked on his hand, pulling him to a stop. He looked back at her, a question in his eyes now. "What's wrong?"

"Heels!" she snapped, pointing down. "I can't walk that fast."

When Emma opened the door for him, Rayed had been stunned anew by the shimmering blue eyes and the tousled look of her hair piled on top of her head. His immediate thought was that he wanted to kiss the base of her neck and inhale the sweet scent of her.

But now that she'd pointed out her shoes, his eyes moved down lower, noticing the way the shimmering, glittery bodice of her cocktail dress hugged her breasts, the impossibly small waist and the floating cascade of the short skirt. She looked...beautiful! Shockingly beautiful! And her legs...they went on forever, ending in shoes that perfectly matched her peach dress. Those tanned legs looked amazing, tempting and taunting him with the dancing hem that ended about mid-thigh. He wondered if she'd worn matching panties and hoped to find out. Did she match her panties and bra? Damn, he wanted to peek!

Later, he reminded himself. She had work to do and he was her escort to accomplish that task. She had a mission and he was simply a tool. He would allow her to use him until they left the party.

Then all bets were off!

"I apologize," Rayed told her, bowing slightly over her hand as he lifted her fingers to his lips. "And may I say how incredibly lovely you look tonight?"

She smiled and those blue eyes glowed. "Yes! And I appreciate the boost to my confidence, sir!" she replied in a flirty tone, adding a saucy little curtsy.

He chuckled softly and placed her hand on his arm, allowing her to lean against him as they descended the stairs to the limousine.

The "yacht" party was in full swing by the time they arrived and it took a great deal of concentration to hide her disappointment that the party was being held at the yacht club beside the marina and not on one of the fabulous ships anchored nearby. This was one of those society events that everyone gossiped about the next day. Anyone who was important, or knew someone who was important, was here in their glittering best. Designers fought to dress the attendees, and the reporters were here, ready to snap photos of anyone daring and important enough to walk down the red carpet.

"You're not going through the receiving line?" Emma asked as the driver of their SUV pulled up to the left of the gaggle of photographers who were literally climbing over each other in an effort to photograph the latest arrival, who was smiling and posing for the cameras.

"I try to avoid the paparazzi," he told her, buttoning his tuxedo jacket before extending his hand to assist her out of the limousine. "It's safer if I don't advertise where I am." Again, he tucked her hand into his elbow, leading her down the sidewalk towards a separate entrance to the restaurant. "Is that a problem?"

She snorted and shook her head. "I'm a reporter, remember? But more importantly, I'm an *undercover* reporter. So, it is better if I don't get my picture and name splashed all over the society pages. Hard to keep one's identity a secret when the paparazzi advertises one's identity."

"I agree," he grumbled, pulling open the door so they could slip into the party unnoticed.

There was a long line of people waiting to get into the event, which was being held in the main dining room of the yacht club. There were flowers everywhere, as well as champagne, and waiters circulated with trays of elaborately prepared appetizers...maybe hors d'oevres? Hmmm...or were they called "*amuse bouche*" at posh parties?

A waiter appeared and presented her artistic offerings, displaying canapés to whoever showed interest. "Pear and honey crostini with candied pecans?" she explained, extending a linen napkin as well.

"This looks delicious!" Emma gushed, pretending to be flighty. She even managed a simper as she nibbled.

Rayed took an appetizer as well, but paused before putting it to his mouth, one dark eyebrow lifted in question at her new persona. Thankfully, he didn't comment until the waiter walked away and they were relatively alone once more.

"Since we were just arguing about the latest environmental legislation coming up for debate, I'm assuming that the simpering giggles are for our audience?"

She smiled and leaned against his chest. Rayed immediately put an arm around her waist, pulling her in closer.

"All for show, my friend."

"Don't even try it," he growled.

Emma blinked, noticing that there were a handful of important politicians, five of them governors from the larger states, laughing together in a corner of the bar. But there was one in particular, the guy who had made the stupid comments about prisoners, who was standing off to the side, head lowered as he conversed with a pair of council members. Two different council members than the men she'd seen him with last night. That was interesting, but not unusual. How often did governors actually chit chat with council members? And why was he arguing with them? Why would the governor argue with council members? And weren't council members too low on the food chain for him to even bother with?

"You're not even with me at this moment, are you?"

Emma blinked and looked up at Rayed. "I'm sorry?"

"What's your interest in the governor?" he asked, his voice low and gravely in her ear. He even paused to nip at the sensitive shell of her ear, which was odd since she'd never even realized that her ear was so sensitive there! What was he playing at?

"Talk to me, Emma," Rayed urged, shifting slightly so that she had a better view of the group of men she was surreptitiously watching. He recognized the governor, a pompous blowhard who had approached him last night about a business opportunity. Their conversation had been cut short when someone had interrupted, so Rayed wasn't entirely sure what the man was up to. But Rayed also knew that the man was as corrupt as they came. The man's hands were downright filthy and Rayed wanted nothing to do with him. That kind of dirt tended to lend a stink to the person, and the governor reeked.

No one had been able to prove that he was into anything shady, though. So if Emma could break through the man's slimy demeanor and reveal him for the corrupt politician that he was, Rayed was all for it. Men like Kevin Mitchell made citizens think all government leaders were corrupt.

Besides, it was fun to watch Emma work the room. And being a part of her investigation seemed like an excellent way for her to learn to trust him.

"What's he doing now?" Emma asked, tilting her head back, acting as if Rayed was saying something fascinating.

"I'm going to turn you around and nibble on your neck." Ah, the benefits of playing a role, he thought as his arm tightened around her waist again. He shifted her carefully and, because of the way he turned her around, his hard thigh pressed between her legs. Because of the flouncy skirt, he was able to enjoy the sensation of her leg nearly straddling him for a brief moment.

Unfortunately, the moment was too brief. Plus, it left both of them more than slightly distracted. He looked down at her and could feel her trembling. "Too much," he growled, his other hand coming around to tighten his hold on her. He could feel her trembling, but couldn't stop the inner groan of satisfaction when she nodded her head slowly. That wasn't fake, he thought with triumph. Emma's reaction just now was real and raw. It was exactly how he felt at the moment and he almost roared when his body responded to her closeness and her trembling reaction.

"Too close and too much," she whispered up to him.

Releasing her, he brought his glass of champagne to his lips and downed it in one gulp, then turned, facing the other guests. He noticed several people eyeing him, but didn't acknowledge them in any way.

He wasn't in the mood to speak with anyone right now. But at that moment, he was reminded of Emma's efforts and looked around. "Why don't we make our way around the room, then end up closer to the governor so that you can eavesdrop?"

"That would be great," she replied, her voice a bit more fluttery than usual. He smiled as he followed through. For the next two hours, he spoke to various guests, not bothering to introduce Emma to anyone. He'd explained earlier that keeping her anonymous and arm candy was all part of the act and she agreed, even playing up on her boredom with the conversation by twirling a finger in her hair occasionally. That helped the gentlemen perceive her as less threatening and, as the alcohol flowed, the conversation loosened up quite a bit.

At one point in the evening, she lifted up onto her toes and he lowered his head as she whispered in his ear, "It's working! Thank you!"

He turned his head and whispered back, "Are you ready to face the governor?"

She leaned back, unconsciously pressing the lower half of her body against his as she peered up at him. "Do you think he's had enough to drink?"

Rayed glanced at the man over her shoulder, careful not to be obvious about it. "I think he's just on the lower side of being completely drunk."

Her grin widened and she nodded. "Excellent!"

He tilted his head slightly. "I have to admit that it's fascinating watching you slip from the ditz to the brainiac, then into the ditz again."

She smiled up at him with a dismissive shrug. "It wouldn't be so easy if men didn't assume a woman was brainless."

"Touché," he laughed. "I'm also enjoying being used as a prop." His lips curled into a sly smile. "I probably shouldn't enjoy it so much, but," his hand slid lower, stopping just above her bottom. She gasped and he laughed softly in her ear. "Exactly why I like being your prop. Definite advantages."

Emma wanted to grab his wrist and pull it higher, but that definitely wouldn't look "right" with the part she was playing. A shiver of excitement went through her and, because she was staring into his eyes, she noticed the intensity ramp up. Thankfully, he didn't move his hand any lower, but nor did he remove it.

"Definite advantages," he repeated, his voice huskier now.

"Your Highness!" a loud voice called out, breaking the growing tension between them.

Emma looked over her shoulder, directly into the eyes of the man she was investigating. For a stunned moment, she wasn't sure what to say. But Rayed took the lead, leaning forward and extending his hand.

"Governor Mitchell. It's a pleasure to finally meet you."

The man puffed up like an idiot. Transferring his glass of bourbon to his other hand, he reached out and shook Rayed's enthusiastically. "It's an honor to meet you as well," the governor replied. "I saw you at last night's party." His gaze washed over Emma. "And your lovely lady as well." He chuckled, letting his eyes slide down Emma's figure and she felt slimy. When his eyes returned to Rayed, he said, "Lucky man. Very lucky indeed!"

Rayed chuckled and looked at Emma with a patronizing grin in his eyes. And immediately, he watched her transform into the bimbo who was flattered by male attention. But he could feel the revulsion in her eyes as the skeevy man surveyed her figure again. This wasn't the same tension he'd felt in her moments ago.

Rayed wanted to pull her close and wrap his arms around her. He wanted to reassure her that he wouldn't let this man drool all over her, even if it was only with his eyes. Hell, he wanted to break the creep's face for daring to stare at Emma in such a proprietary manner! How dare he survey her like that, as if he had the right!

Emma must have recognized his anger, because she touched his chest lightly, bringing his attention back to her.

"I agree," he said, finally remembering that the governor had said he was lucky. Slowly, only because of Emma's touch, did the anger ease.

"I heard about the new utility proposals that are coming up for a vote in your state, Governor Mitchell," Rayed said. "Have you considered shifting more resources to solar energy? We've moved towards solar in Fahre and it's been quite beneficial."

The governor chuckled. "Isn't your country one of the largest oil producing countries in the world? I thought the majority of your income came from oil revenues. Why would you transition to solar?"

Rayed refrained from rolling his eyes at the stupid question. "You're correct that most of our revenue is currently derived from oil sales. But we're using that revenue to expand our education systems. An educated population is now creating brilliant ideas for the future."

"Yes, yes," the governor agreed too quickly, shifting on his feet as if bored. "But it's pretty damn nice to have such easy revenue, right?"

Emma sighed and looked away, acting bored with the conversation. She tilted her glass of champagne to her lips, but didn't drink anything. She held the glass there for a long moment, pretending to be guzzling the drink.

The men were discussing something else now and Emma looked away, still leaning casually against Rayed and pretending to be admiring the various dresses the other women were wearing, when in reality, she was listening hard. Pulling her phone out of her purse, she flipped through the various apps, still going for the bored attitude. In reality, she was flipping to her phone's recorder.

With a hefty sigh, she turned to press her body against Rayed's. "I'm going to the little girl's room," she purred, then lifted up onto her toes to kiss his jaw. A moment later, she slipped out of his arms, all the while, Emma used her hidden hand to slip her cell phone into Rayed's pocket.

They might not say anything while she was gone, but she didn't want to take any chances. The governor was doing something nefarious, she just knew it! She just needed to prove it!

Emma sashayed away, but paused to peek back over her shoulder, giving Rayed a sly look and praying that others might interpret her glance as flirtatious. When he winked in her direction, she giggled and walked towards the bathrooms.

The bathrooms were up a long, marble staircase and Emma silently groaned at the number of steps. Her poor feet were not going to like this! It's not as if she actually needed to use the restroom. But she'd wanted to give Governor Mitchell time to make Rayed an offer. Not that it was a guarantee that Mitchell would bring Rayed into the business deal. It was a risk she'd had to take.

In the bathroom, she touched up her lipstick and dumped the champagne down the drain. It would help her image if she had to get a fresh glass when she reappeared by Rayed's side. Thankfully, it was early enough in the evening that the bathrooms were still empty. In about two hours, after everyone had been drinking, the bathrooms would be significantly busier.

She started to reach for her phone to check the time, but then remembered that she'd left it in Rayed's pocket. "Right!" she groaned, then turned and walked out of the bathroom.

The hallway was as empty as the bathroom, so she took a moment to slip her shoes off, padding barefoot down the carpeted hallway. It was only a short moment of respite from the torture of her heels, but helped a lot! At the top of the marble staircase, she paused, gripping the railing as she bent to slip her shoes back on.

Because she was busy putting her feet back into her heels, Emma was caught off balance when a hard shove came from behind! Emma cried out, her hand tightening on the railing as she tumbled forward, trying, and failing, to stop herself from falling headfirst into the hard, stone stairs. Her shoulder slammed into the railing, as she pitched forward, hitting her head on the marble step hard enough to see stars. And then more pain erupted as her hip, elbow, and knee hit the steps just as hard

and at equally awkward and painful angles.
For some reason, the dragon from her nightmare last night flashed before her eyes, but she was too intent on trying to stop herself from falling further down the stairs.
When she finally came to a halt at the bottom, silence all around her, Emma closed her eyes as pain made itself known throughout her body. Blinking up at the ornate ceiling, she wondered if she'd broken anything. Carefully, she wiggled her fingers. They all moved, although slowly. That was a good sign, right?
Okay, fingers were good. Legs?
"Emma!" Rayed's deep voice called out. A moment later, he was beside her, holding her hand while he checked her over for injuries.

Rayed couldn't believe his eyes. Emma, his beautiful, courageous Emma, was sprawled on the floor at the bottom of the stairs. She'd fallen in those ridiculous heels!
He turned to the nearest of his guards. "Call an ambulance!" he snapped.
"No!" she whispered weakly. "No ambulance!"
His lips thinned as he pressed a hand to the side of her head. "Emma, you just fell down the stairs. Where does it hurt?"
He wanted to pick her up and cradle her, sooth all the pain away from her eyes. He wanted to wrap his arms around her and make her feel better somehow! But he didn't do any of those things, terrified that she'd broken a bone and moving her would make it worse.
"I'm fine," she whispered and there was a small rush of relief when she spoke. However, she clearly wasn't fine. She was hurt, damn it! She'd fallen down the marble steps! He wanted to snap the stupid heels right off those shoes.
"You're *not* fine," he growled, seeing the goose egg already swelling on her forehead. "You banged your head pretty badly. You need to go to the hospital."
Emma groaned, but she moved her arms, slowly at first, then her legs. He tugged the floaty dress down to cover more of her glorious thighs, not because he didn't want others to see her legs, but because he was too distracted by those legs! And shame filled him. She was injured and he was distracted and aroused by her legs!
"No, I'm fine," she told him, but he heard her groan quietly as she tried to sit up.
"Hold still, love," he urged, putting a hand to her shoulder to stop her.
Unfortunately, the daft woman used his hand as leverage to pull herself into a sitting position. That alleviated a small bit of his terror, since

she was able to move both arms and her legs.

"I'm fine," she repeated. He didn't believe her. Not with that huge knot forming on her forehead. "I just need a moment to...to..." she blinked and he panicked even more.

"Ambulance!" Rayed snarled.

"Please!" she whispered, putting a hand to his arm. It stopped his words as well as his thoughts.

One of his body guards leaned forward. "Your Highness, there's a traffic accident three miles from here that has blocked traffic from getting through. The ambulance won't reach us for another fifteen minutes."

Rayed snarled, then reached down to lift her into his arms. "We'll take her to the hospital!" he announced. "Get the car around. Now!"

The guards were already running towards the doors, pushing them open and speaking rapidly into their hidden microphones.

"My dress!" Emma gasped, then reached underneath her to pull her flirty skirt down, valiantly trying to hide her panties. Rayed didn't understand her horror until he glanced down at her. He'd lifted her up into his arms, one arm behind her back and the other under her knees. If she'd been wearing a longer skirt, it could have been tucked under her knees. But the skirt on this cocktail dress was too short.

He almost laughed out loud with relief. If she was concerned about flashing someone, then she wasn't as badly hurt as he'd thought.

"No one will see your...uh..." He wasn't quite sure what words to use. Panties? If she was wearing a thong, as so many of his previous mistresses had preferred, then no one would see her panties at all. They'd sure see her bum though!

Now why did the thought of her lovely bum make him even more aroused? She was hurt and he couldn't even slow his lust down long enough to make certain she was okay?

He was going to hell, he thought in disgust. Thankfully, only his guards were in the hallway. One of which already had the inconspicuous exit door open and, at the end of a short sidewalk, his driver waited with the door to the SUV open.

Briefly, he nodded his gratitude, then ducked into the backseat, cradling Emma on his lap.

"I'm fine," she whispered, but he felt her lean her head against his shoulder as the SUV began moving away from the yacht club and towards the hospital.

"You're not fine," he replied, tightening his arms around her. But he immediately loosened them again when she gasped in pain. "What's wrong? Did I hurt you?"

"I don't know," she replied, lifting her fingers to delicately touch her head.

"Don't," he warned, grabbing her hand. "You have a vicious knot on your forehead. You must have hit it pretty hard when you fell."

For some odd reason, he felt her still as a blank look washed over her face. "What's wrong?"

"I didn't fall, Rayed," she whispered urgently. She'd tried to be quiet, but the guards sitting in the front seat heard her, the one in the passenger seat turning his head slightly to hear her better. "Someone pushed me."

Everyone in the vehicle seemed to still at her words. Then the group started to move quickly. The driver sped up the vehicle and the guard in the passenger seat began muttering low and quickly into his microphone. A dark SUV pulled up right next to them, which startled Emma. "What's that?"

"That's another one of my guard vehicles," Rayed assured her, tightening his arms around her ever so slightly. His voice was low and, when she looked up at him, his eyes stared straight ahead, his jaw clenched tightly.

"I'm sorry," she whispered and tried to scoot off his lap.

Rayed didn't let her move. His hand settled on top of her thigh, the other arm still around her back.

"Don't," was all he said. His hands were gentle, but she knew that they would be firm if she tried to move again. And since her head was throbbing so painfully that she was almost sick with it, she leaned her head against his shoulder again. The tears were unexpected. Emma rarely cried. She considered tears to be pointless. When something saddened her, she would allow the emotion to wash over her, then figure out how to fix it.

Unfortunately, her defenses were low because of the pain. And fear. Someone had just tried to kill her. And if she were completely honest with herself, she was also hurt that Rayed seemed angry with her. She didn't understand his reaction, but it hurt her deep down inside in places she hadn't realized were vulnerable to his opinion.

By now, the pain was a living thing and she lifted her nose higher, breathing in Rayed's scent gratefully. It relaxed her, which eased the pain ever so slightly. It still throbbed, but with her nose pressed against his neck, she could at least manage the pain..

Rayed felt the tickling of her nose against his neck and even that turned him on. He couldn't believe that she was in pain and he was throbbing with need for her. What an ass I am, he thought!

And the idea that someone had deliberately hurt her, probably someone trying to get to him through her, caused a rage to build up inside of him unlike anything he'd ever felt before. He wanted to tighten his arms around her, to tell her that he'd never allow anything to hurt her, ever again. He wanted to get out of this limousine and find whoever had pushed her down the stairs, then pummel that person with his bare fists until the man, or woman, could never push anyone ever again.

Breathing in slowly, he tried to calm himself down. A rage this intense wouldn't help Emma in any way. He had to think, had to find evidence or make the connections in the conversations he'd had with people this evening that would provide information to his guards, so that they could figure out what had happened to Emma.

Carefully, he lifted a hand, wanting to stroke her hair, but stopped, worried that she might have other head injuries that he wasn't aware of. She was in so much pain; the last thing he wanted to do was make it worse.

Thankfully, his driver finally pulled up to the emergency room entrance. Someone had obviously called ahead, because two orderlies and a nurse were standing by with a wheel chair, ready to assist Emma out of the vehicle.

"This isn't necessary," she objected, but Rayed ignored her and set her gently down into the chair.

"We'll take very good care of her," the nurse said.

Rayed knew that the comment was meant to both reassure him and also let him know that they were taking her away. That simply wasn't going to happen! "I'm going with her."

The orderlies were already pushing the chair into the hospital, but the nurse stepped in his way. "Are you related to her, sir?"

Rayed wanted to roar with fury. "No, but..."

"Then I'm sorry, sir, but we must maintain her privacy."

He gave the woman his darkest scowl. "I'm going in there!"

The nurse chuckled, but gently shook her head. "As soon as the doctor has evaluated her injuries, I will come and get you. But if you're in the exam room, you'll only slow the doctor down." She put a comforting hand on his arm. "I promise I'll get you as soon as she asks for you, sir. But please let us help her first, okay?"

Rayed rubbed a hand over his face, anger and frustration boiling inside of him. "Fine!" he grumbled, but only because he didn't want to stop anything that might help Emma feel better.

His guards formed a perimeter around him as he paced around the waiting room. The area was fairly empty this early in the evening, but even so, one of his guards must have called the hospital administrator because Rayed and his team were eventually led into a private waiting area and someone came to update him every fifteen minutes.

So, when the original nurse arrived and beamed in his direction, Rayed breathed a sigh of relief.

"She's going to be fine," she assured him. "She has a very bad concussion and the doctor wants to admit her for observation." Rayed drew breath to argue, but she lifted her hands to stop him, "Only in an overabundance of caution, Your Highness," she assured him. Damn it, he hated that someone had given this woman his identity. Or maybe, he *wasn't* angry about it. If it meant they'd tell him what he needed to know, he didn't give a damn who knew who he was.

"We'll monitor her overnight and have more information for you in the morning."

Rayed was already shaking his head before she finished that last statement. "She's coming with me. She won't be safe here at the hospital." He paused and looked at the nurse. "Nor will your staff. I don't have the personnel here that can protect everyone."

The nurse opened her mouth to argue, but at his glare, she relented and nodded slowly. "I understand," she replied, her voice quiet now as the implication of what he'd just said sunk into her mind. She took a slow, deep breath, then explained, "I'll have one of the orderlies bring her to you. Is there someone who can watch over her tonight?"

One of the guards stepped forward, telling the nurse what Rayed didn't have the patience to explain. "I have a doctor on standby," the guard explained.

For the first time in his life, Rayed was glad to have his guards around him, ready to step in to say and do what was needed. Because the relief that there was no long-lasting harm to Emma was so intense, he felt dizzy. Reaching out, he gripped the back of one of the uncomfortable waiting room chairs, letting his relief wash over him.

By the time he was able to think properly, the nurse was gone. Damn, he had more questions. But they would have to wait. He needed to ask Emma questions. That was paramount.

The doctor arrived to explain Emma's concussion, basically repeating the information from the nurse. Emma would need lots of sleep and someone to watch her tonight, looking for warning signs. The doctor warned Rayed that it would be a long night if he stayed with Emma, but there was no way he could leave Emma alone. Not after what she'd gone through.

"No broken bones?"

The doctor shook his head. "No. No broken bones, but she's going to feel every one of those bruises, and probably some strained muscles by the morning." He waved in the direction of the emergency room area, then continued. "She suffered a severely strained wrist, so we've stabilized that for now. And her shoulder is badly bruised, so she'll need to take it easy for a few days, maybe a week, to let the shoulder heal. She suffered several deep contusions and," the doctor adjusted his language at Rayed's sudden panic. "Just deep bruises, Your Highness," he explained, then continued, "which means she'll need to relax for at least several days to let her body heal."

"I'll make sure that happens," Rayed assured the doctor.

"The real problem is the concussion. On the way down the stairs, she hit her head several times." He looked down at the patient file, then up to Rayed. "Does she have a friend or family member who can be with her tonight?" Emma arrived in a wheelchair, looking beautiful and bruised. But Rayed couldn't look at her. Not yet. He'd seen a glimpse of her head wrapped in a bandage, plus another around her left wrist. Seeing her wounded like this made his blood boil with fury. He needed to remain rational so that he understood how to help her heal.

"I'll stay with her," Rayed announced, not bothering to look at Emma, because he knew she'd object. "Does she need to be woken every couple of hours?"

The doctor looked at Emma, shaking his head. "No. That used to be the case. However, we've found that sleep is more important to heal the body. But keep her awake for the next few hours. If she has any slurred speech or dizziness, contact me immediately." The doctor scribbled something on Emma's chart, then stuffed his pen into his coat pocket. "After tonight, she'll need lots of sleep, and I'll give her a prescription for pain medication, just in case her wrist or shoulder pain become too much."

"I'll make certain that she takes the medicine."

"Will you now?" Emma asked, her tone soft and sweet, but her eyes gave away her irritation.

Rayed glanced at her, then quickly away. He wasn't going to let her softness interfere with his concentration again. He needed to protect her! If someone had tried to hurt her by getting to him, then he had to be better at protecting her.

"I will," he asserted to the doctor, ignoring Emma's growl. Rayed wasn't sure if he should interpret that sound as her objecting to his assertion that he'd take care of her, or if she was in pain.

The doctor wrote something down on Emma's chart, then flipped it closed with a firm nod. "Okay, then that's it. Take the pain meds as needed, but if the pain becomes too much for my prescription to manage, see your personal physician or come back here to the emergency room." He looked firmly at Emma. "If you feel uncertain in *any* way, I can admit you to the hospital."

Rayed understood that the doctor was trying to silently communicate that, if she was being abused, she had an escape route. At least for one night.

Emma grasped what he was implying as well. She smiled encouragingly at the doctor as she said, "This truly was just a tumble down the stairs, Doctor. Thank you so much for your help."

Finally, they were alone. Since they were in a private exam room, not even the sounds from the emergency department filtered in. There was just silence. And that ever-present tension.

"Thank you," she whispered.

"For what?"

"For taking care of me."

A knock on the door interrupted whatever he might have said next. Rayed's expression turned to a scowl, but he pulled open the door only to have an arm appear, holding out a bag. "*Shukran lak*," he said with gratitude to the mysterious person. Rayed took it and closed the door again, turning to hand the bag to her.

"I had my staff find more comfortable clothes for you," he explained.

Emma was so startled by his thoughtfulness that it took her a moment to accept the bag. She noticed the uncomfortable expression wash over Rayed's face and wondered if he had ever asked for his staff to obtain clothing for anyone before. Surely, he'd bought clothing for his mistresses in the past, hadn't he?

Still, the gesture was so thoughtful, so wonderful, that she hugged the bag to her chest, smiling up at him instead of peering into the bag. "Thank you," she whispered to him, then grabbed his jacket with one hand, pulling him down to her level. "Thank you!" she whispered in a more urgent tone a moment before she kissed him.

The kiss was meant to be just a brief brush of her lips against his, but the moment their lips touched, a surge of need bubbled up between them. Emma wasn't sure if it was her instigation, or his, but someone groaned and he leaned forward, deepening the kiss. It went on for several moments, or maybe longer, until his hand reached up to cup the back of her head, inadvertently pressing against one of the lumps caused by her fall. She yelped, cringing as she gritted her teeth to ride out the pain lashing at her head. Closing her eyes, she tried to relax her muscles and let the pain ease.

When she could open her eyes again, it was to find a concerned nurse standing in front of her with a small, plastic cup that contained two white pills, and a glass of water.

"Better?" the nurse asked, his eyes moving over her face as if assessing her level of pain.

Emma slowly, carefully, nodded her head.

"Your husband asked us to get some pain meds immediately so you don't have to wait until he could get the prescription filled." He lifted the small cup. "Ready to take them now?"

"Yes!" Emma hissed and took the pills, popping them into her mouth before taking a long sip of the cold water. "Thank you!"

The nurse smiled encouragingly. "That should help, but be sure and fill that prescription so you can keep ahead of the pain. The meds might make you sleepy. Don't fight the feeling. Your body needs rest in order to recover."

"Will do," Emma assured the kind nurse as he left the room.

Alone again with Rayed, she looked around, and gazed despondently down at the bag of clothes that had fallen to the floor. Rayed bent down and picked up the bag, setting it beside her on the exam table. "Why don't you change clothes and I'll wait outside for you?" He lightly ran a finger over her cheek. "I'll take better care of you, *habitat alqalb*." A moment later, he was gone, giving her the privacy she needed to get dressed.

Emma sat there for a long moment, warmed by his soft touch and wondering what "*habitat alqalb*" meant. He'd done so much for her! The clothes, the medicine, and the visit to the emergency room. The man was incredibly wonderful, she thought as she peered into the bag.

"Oh goodness!" she whispered as she pulled out a pair of drawstring pants, and hugged them to her chest. "Perfect!" There was also a soft sweatshirt and socks and...whoever had gotten these clothes was brilliant...sneakers! They were so comfortable. By the time she was changed, she felt significantly better. The pain meds probably helped as well, she thought with a smile as she dumped the cocktail dress into the bag. She looked around for her shoes, but they weren't there. She must have lost them at the yacht club, she thought with a grimace. The shoes had been only four dollars, but Amanda wasn't going to appreciate their loss! It was hard to find shoes that match peach dresses!

"I'll find them tomorrow," she told herself as she looked around for her purse and phone. "Oh no!"

Jerking the door open, she searched for and found Rayed. He must have been waiting for her to open the door. "What's wrong?"

"My purse!" she whispered. "I don't have my purse with me. It has my phone and wallet in it."

He shook his head. "I didn't stop to find your purse," he admitted, as he pulled something out of his pocket. "But I have your phone here. You slipped it into my pocket right before you left to use the restroom."

"Oh thank you!" she gushed, suddenly remembering how she'd hoped to record the conversation with Governor Mitchell.

"He didn't say anything important," Rayed assured her, taking her elbow and leading her out of the closest hospital exit. "But I have a breakfast meeting with him tomorrow morning."

That was a surprise! "You do?"

"Yes," Rayed replied, nodding sharply. "And I suspect that he'll reveal a bit more about his utility plans."

"Excellent. And," she smiled brightly up at him, thinking that the pain medication was wonderful, "do you need a date for that meal, by any chance?"

He looked down at her as the SUV came to a smooth halt in front of them. "We'll see how you feel in the morning. If you aren't any better," he looked at her sternly, "and I mean *much* better without the pain meds, then I'll record the conversation for you."

Emma suspected that was the best she was going to get, but she still smiled her gratitude. "Thank you!"

"Let's go. You're coming back with me. I'm going to make sure that you rest tonight. I've already called your roommate to let her know what's going on."

She lifted startled eyes up to him, pausing as she was about to step into the SUV. "You called Amanda?"

"Yes. She wasn't worried at the time, but I suspected that she might be even more anxious if you didn't come home tonight."

She was just about to get into the backseat when his words struck her. "I'm not going home tonight?"

"Nope," he replied, as he settled her in the seat before getting in himself. "You're coming with me so that I can watch over you tonight. If you have any problems, my guards can get you to the emergency room faster than an ambulance."

Emma considered that for a moment. They were driving swiftly through the darkened city streets and she wondered what might happen if she went with him tonight. Since he was holding her hand, he felt her shiver of anticipation. Still conscious of the guards sitting in the front seat, Emma licked her lips, trying to figure out how she could tell him what she wanted. It was a simple answer; him. She wanted Rayed.

"Mitchell, I heard that you have some...advantageous...business opportunities," Hammel Caruthers commented as he strolled over to the pompous governor. Hammel prided himself on finding excellent business opportunities and he didn't concern himself with ethics or legalities. He was a businessman and had enough backing to ensure that, if there were any legal issues, his team of very expensive lawyers could get him out of any situation, no matter how sticky.

Mitchell turned, smiling when he recognized the wealthy billionaire. "I always have exciting opportunities, depending on the investor in question."

Hammel rolled his eyes, struggling for patience. "Look Mitchell, I heard about the internet thing you've got going. From what I understand, you have the authority to nominate the members for the board of directors for the internet board, then your state's senate will approve your nominees. Right now, you have two more appointees to put into place, then you're moving forward with the plan." He gestured towards a group of chairs set away from the other people that were still milling about at the late night party. More than half of the guests had left the yacht club. Some of them had gone off to their own yachts if they were moored in this exclusive marina. Others might have headed to another party, and some had simply gone home. Since it was just after one o'clock in the morning, Mitchell thought of the others as wimps. Most of the more interesting parties didn't get started until around two o'clock, when the bars closed down.

Hammel might suspect about Mitchell's very interesting party with five or six other people that were now waiting on his presence. A *very* exclusive party, he thought. A party in which the governor could do all the things that he craved with the men he craved.

Mitchell surveyed the handsome businessman, wondering what the billionaire's preferences might be. Unfortunately, the man preferred the ladies. Pity.

However, if Hammel was interested in discussing business, Mitchell was more than happy to hang around to reel the man into the opportunity.

Both men sat heavily in the chairs set away from everyone else, providing a bit of privacy. They'd shucked their tuxedo jackets long ago and each had a drink in hand.

"So, what do you know?" Kevin asked, taking a sip of his bourbon.

Hammel shifted impatiently in his chair. "I know you've got the board of directors nearly set up. I know that you have already drafted legislation that would allow your internet company to..."

"I don't have any stock in that internet company," Kevin interrupted.

Hammel rolled his eyes. "Mitchell, we both know that you don't need to own actual stock in the company to make a profit. So stop putzing with me." He toyed with the crystal glass, clinking the ice cubes against the crystal. "I know this draft legislation will allow your internet buddies," he continued, clarifying the situation, "to move in to certain areas and offer low cost internet, substantially beating out the competition."

"There's nothing illegal about it," Kevin filled in during the silence. "As governor of my state, a cheaper alternative to an essential utility is–"

"Careful, Mitchell," Hammel warned softly. "Speaking of the internet as an essential utility would put the internet companies under a different jurisdiction and would allow that federal agency to put more oversight onto the business."

Keven chuckled, nodding his head. "Good point." He took a sip of bourbon, cleared his throat and continued. "As governor, I am always looking for ways to help my voters receive better and more cost effective services." He paused, lifting an eyebrow until Hammel chuckled approvingly before continuing. "Once the competition is undercut enough that the other internet companies move out of the initial areas, there is the possibility of a substantial price increase."

More ice shaking as Hammel glared at Kevin. Finally, he asked, "And you have enough of those ridiculous, headline grabbing proposed legislation ideas queued up to distract any reporter that might get too close to the real issue?"

"Absolutely," Kevin snickered.

"Are they good enough to make the parents take action and cause the other special interest groups go bonkers? Even though your stupid proposals are answers to problems that don't even exist?"

Kevin laughed, throwing his head back. "I have enough ideas to make even your head spin, Hammel." He took another sip of his bourbon, feeling good. If he could reel Hammel in and maybe one more big investor, they'd have a solid group in place.

Hammel seemed to be considering the opportunity, but Kevin knew the bastard was all in. He loved schemes like this. The guy's business dealings were almost as corrupt as Kevin's governorship! And they both knew this was how legacies were made!

Not that Mitchell cared if he left anything to his kids. The wife and kids were merely a necessary evil for anyone in politics.

Impatiently, Kevin stood up, glancing at his watch even though he knew exactly what time it was. It was just a power move. "I have to be somewhere in a few minutes, Hammel." He drained his glass, then set it on the railing for the wait staff to collect. Yeah, he could have set the glass down on the table nearby where the rest of the empty glasses from the evening were resting, waiting to be taken to the kitchens for cleaning, but this was another power move. Governors didn't bring their dirty glasses to the wait staff. The wait staff came to him! "Let me know if you're in or out."

And then he left, salivating in anticipation of the next "party". Yeah, he was done with business for the night. Now it was time to have some fun!

Chapter 5

"I feel fine," Emma muttered, barely able to keep her eyes open. Her head felt heavy, so she leaned her head against Rayed's broad shoulder because...well, wasn't that the whole point of having broad shoulders? Yep, they were a place to rest one's head, she thought with a happy sigh.

"I like your shoulders," she mumbled, already more than half asleep.

She felt Rayed's arms tighten gently around her. "I'm relieved you approve."

"Approve?" she asked, trying to perk up. She suspected that his comment was important, but she was just too tired. Stupid medicine! It was making her sleepy. There was something important that she needed to tell him. Something she couldn't quite remember. The medicine wasn't just making her sleepy. It was making her head fuzzy. Or was the fuzziness caused by her sleepiness?

That question was too complicated just now. She sighed again and snuggled closer.

"I could get used to this," she muttered against his chest.

"That's a good thing for our future then," Rayed's deep voice replied. Did he laugh after that comment? She'd have to be very stern with him tomorrow if he was! Shame on him for laughing!

Yawning, Emma tried valiantly to stay awake. That thing, that forgotten issue, was pinging the back of her head. She needed to tell him something, something very important. But the bed she was laid down upon was incredibly soft! And the blanket warmed her almost as much as the warm body behind her back. A heavy arm draped over her waist and...she was out.

Rayed held Emma in his arms, not moving for fear of waking her up.

Every few minutes, he raised his head slightly to listen to her breathing. Then he'd relax back against the pillows again, staring at the ceiling. Sleep evaded him, but that wasn't surprising. Emma's soft butt kept rubbing against his erection, never letting him forget how painfully he wanted to make love to her.

He wouldn't, because he knew she was in a great deal of pain. Her wrist was bandaged and there were two large lumps on her head. Her shoulder wasn't swollen, but he knew that it pained her as well since she'd been protecting it as they left the hospital.

Someone had pushed his Emma down the stairs. The biggest question; had they hurt her as a way to get to him? Or had they hurt her because of her job?

He wasn't sure, but he was damned sure going to protect her. No one was going to harm Emma again!

Rayed knew that he should get up and consult with his guards. But the need to hold Emma, to feel her breathing as she slept, was too strong. So instead of doing what he should do, for the first time in a long time, he did what he wanted to do. He closed his eyes and held Emma close. He wouldn't sleep. Not tonight. Not with her feeling so perfect in his arms. But it was enough to just close his eyes.

Chapter 6

Emma woke with a start and looked around. The room wasn't her bedroom. Not even close! The soft, teal walls and the silver accents were beautiful, but this room was enormous! Her entire apartment could fit inside this one room!

And the bed was incredibly soft. Her bed at home was lumpy, but until she could afford a new mattress, the lumps were there to stay.

There was a warmth against her back too. A heaviness that wasn't familiar. Could the warmth be...?

She swiveled her head so that she could see who was behind her, then hissed as pain lashed across her forehead. It wasn't as bad as last night, but it still hurt!

"Easy," Rayed's sleep-roughened voice soothed as he gently pulled her back down beside him. With one hand, he rubbed her back, kneading the tense muscles in her shoulders. When she relaxed again, he got out of bed and headed for the bathroom, coming back with some pills.

Emma closed her eyes, holding up a hand. "No, I don't want more of the pain meds. I got too sleepy and..." she rubbed her forefinger over her forehead. "I need to remember something. And whatever that medication was, it helped the pain, but it also made my mind all fuzzy. I can't seem to remember what I was trying to think of last night."

Without saying a word, Rayed walked back into the bathroom, returning a moment later with another medicine.

Before she could shake her head, he explained, "This is just acetaminophen. It won't make you sleepy or cause your thoughts to become muddled."

Emma hesitated, then reached for the pills, washing them down with the water he offered.

He put the glass of water back on the bedside table, then got back into the bed. He was currently only wearing a pair of jeans that rode low on his hips. Had he worn those last night? She pushed through the memories from last night and this morning, blushing when she came to the conclusion that no, he hadn't been wearing them last night. She vaguely remembered waking up at some point during the night to feel his naked body against hers. Thankfully, she was still dressed and... wait a minute. She didn't have those comfy drawstring pants on anymore.

"I took them off last night to make you more comfortable," he explained, somehow reading her mind as he pulled her into his arms, carefully placing her head on his chest. "How does the rest of your body feel?"

On fire? Ready to ravish the man holding her so gently in his arms? Oh yeah!

"Your wrist?" he asked, lifting her hand up in the air

It took her brain several moments to shift her concentration to her wrist when he held her like this. "I think it's fine," she finally told him.

"You think?" he prompted, running a finger along the sensitive skin on the underside of her forearm.

She cleared her throat and pulled her hand away. "I can't think straight when you're touching me, Rayed," she admitted.

"Is that so?" he asked. She couldn't see him, but Emma could hear the smile in his voice.

"Don't get cocky on me."

"Too late."

Too late for...? Oh! A glance lower clearly showed what he meant. The erection was straining against the denim of his jeans. A very impressive erection, she thought! Goodness, her fingers itched to smooth down over that bulge, to explore and discover what he looked like without the denim.

"You're killing me, Emma," he groaned, as he rolled over, carefully tucking her underneath him.

"What was I doing?"

He lowered his head, nuzzling her neck until she gasped. Lower, he shifted his hips so that she was cradling him with her hips, her legs wrapped around his waist.

"You were looking and wondering," he growled as he moved to the other side of her neck. "I'm going to kiss you and you're not going to move. And if I do anything that hurts, or if I start to do something that you're not ready for, tell me to stop, okay?"

Emma sighed with relief. "Yes," she whispered, wishing she could sound more confident. But the idea of him kissing her, or doing something he thought she might not be ready for, seemed like a delicious plan!

Sneaky hands were already underneath the sweatshirt and she gasped when those fingers cupped her breasts through her bra. When his fingers curled around her breasts, tweaking the nipples slightly, it felt amazing, better than anything she'd ever experienced. It probably helped that he was still kissing her neck, nibbling at her ear lobe, and teasing the shell of her ear. Her non-bandaged hand curled into his hair, feeling the soft strands on a man where nothing else was soft.

As his hands explored, tweaking her nipples, she gasped and shifted against him.

"No moving, Emma," he ordered, his voice raspy now. "The pain pill probably hasn't kicked in yet."

"But..."

He nipped her earlobe. "Just relax and let me explore your body, okay?"

"Okay," she sighed, but wasn't sure if she could just lay back and not move. That seemed...impossible. Especially when those fingers smoothed back and forth over her taut nipple, driving her wild with need. Her hips couldn't remain still and her legs tightened around his hips, pressing her core against that shockingly nice, impressively large erection still constrained behind his jeans.

"Rayed!" she gasped when he pinched her nipple. She closed her eyes, savoring the delicious pleasure. Thankfully, the pain reliever had finally kicked in and there was only a faint throb on her forehead when she moved. Besides, whatever Rayed was doing to her breasts was so much nicer than worrying about her headache! The man's fingers were magic! And his tongue! Dear heaven, his tongue! What in the world was he doing to her neck!

"Don't move," he soothed again, then moved lower, his hands pushing her sweatshirt higher up to bare her stomach.

For several moments, his fingertips grazed back and forth over her stomach and her body came down from the crazy high of moments before. She opened her eyes to look at him.

"Are you okay?" he asked, real concern in his eyes.

"Yes!" she replied, trying to convey how very "okay" she was.

"Do you want me to stop?"

"No!" she gasped, almost sitting up in alarm. "Please don't stop!"

He laughed, then ducked his head to kiss her lightly. "I don't want to stop, but tell me if your head starts hurting, okay?"

"Yes!" she replied, but Emma wasn't sure if she was agreeing, or if the yes was because his hands moved higher, returning to her breasts.

She'd thought her body had calmed down? Nope! It was just simmering while he teased her stomach.

Another husky laugh was her only warning before he ducked his head, his hot mouth covering her nipple and she cried out, arching up into his mouth. She loved it and...yeah, he needed to stop that because it was making her head spin with desire.

And yet, when he looked up at her, she whimpered and pushed his head back down, his mouth latching onto her nipple, that magical tongue flicking against the sensitive peak. Another whimper and she couldn't seem to stop her body from grinding against his. There was a small increase in the throbbing pain in her head, but Emma ignored it, wanting this more than she wanted to avoid the pain.

"I love the noises you make, Emma," he groaned and moved his mouth even lower.

His fingers trailed along her thighs, making her shiver. Her bare thighs! That throbbing part of her was covered only by her satin panties. His finger skimmed along her thighs, making an infuriating pattern that brought him closer and closer to her desperately throbbing core.

"You're a tease," she gasped, shifting her hips in an unconscious enticement.

His only response was a grumbly laugh. But then he lowered his head, kissing her inner thighs. "You are beautiful, Emma," he growled.

"Right. Beautiful." She closed her eyes, wishing that he would move faster. Her body was throbbing in anticipation and Emma knew that she'd never been a particularly patient person.

"You're also very fun to tease."

Emma wanted to scream! "You're such a jerk!" The words were harsh, but her playful tone indicated otherwise.

Rayed smiled, his eyes moving to that satin covered core of his woman. "Harsh words will only slow me down, *habitat alqalb*."

Emma arched her back, her feminine scent filling his nostrils, making his body throb with the need to thrust into her. But he knew that patience, teasing Emma and bringing her body to a deeper arousal, would be better in the long term. He wanted to feel her body tremble under his mouth and pulse around his shaft. His goal took time and patience. Plus, understanding her body was essential to their long term happiness.

Her fingers dove back into his hair and he smiled again. Damn, she was so hot! He loved the silent pleading.

He slid her panties slowly down her legs. He tossed them out of the way, then resumed teasing the inside of her thighs. Such perfectly pale thighs, he thought.

"I'm going to smack you!" she grumbled.

"Think so?" he teased. He gazed up at her, enjoying this more than he'd thought possible. "With what, *habibi*?" He kissed the top of her mound while his forefinger teased the wetness at her opening. He heard her gasp, but his eyes were focused on those delicious, tempting pink folds. She looked like dessert! "One hand is in a splint and your other hand is attached to a sore shoulder."

"Rayed!" Emma groaned, her head dropping back onto the mattress, her body writhing, desperate for his touch.

She was ready, he thought and slid his finger into her. Her inner muscles instantly tightened and he had to pause to regain control of himself. Between that tightness and her delicious scent, he was riding the razor's edge of his control.

He licked lightly while his finger turned, tickling the upper side of her body. Rayed was too absorbed in his task to concern himself with her screams of pleasure. He ignored her fingers pulling at his hair as well. He was going to enjoy this and he wouldn't allow Emma to rush him.

With another flick of his tongue against that perfect nub, he watched admiringly as her body glistened. But the temptation was too much and he moved closer, his mouth and tongue exploring her, tasting her, discovering all the small ways that made her gasp or moan. Every new bit of information, he tucked away as precious knowledge.

Finally, he gave her the release that he knew she craved. Putting his mouth over that nub, he sucked hard while his fingers teased from the inside, sliding in and out while his tongue flicked against her button. It took only moments before her release overwhelmed her, leaving her gasping.

Rayed eased up the pressure, but kept teasing that nub to give her as much pleasure as possible. But when her screams eased into soft, wispy sighs, he couldn't hold back any longer. He grabbed a condom from the bedside table and rolled it down over his now-painful erection. Moving back to her, he positioned himself between her legs.

"Tell me to stop if I hurt you," he groaned, sliding into her body. He closed his eyes as the pleasure from her tightness almost caused him to climax right then and there. It had been a while, he thought hazily, not sure when the last time he'd been with a woman was. In fact, his brain fizzled completely. Everything was about pleasure now.

Thrusting slowly, he brought her body back to life. Her gasp of delight encouraged him further. Her legs lifted, wrapping around his waist and that movement pulled him even deeper within her body. He groaned, closing his eyes to hold on just a little longer. But she was just too tight, too wet, and so incredibly hot! Faster and faster, he thrust into her. When he knew that his body was dangerously close to losing control, so he shifted so he could tease that sensitive nub with his thumb.

That was all it took to bring her over the edge again and he thrust faster, roaring his pleasure as his body shuddered with release. He held her as gently as possible, but he felt as if his soul was pouring out of him. Never had the pleasure been this intense, this all-consuming, before.

And when it was all over, he barely had the strength to not drop on top of her. He shifted to the side, praying that he wasn't hurting her as he stared up at the ceiling.

Rayed wanted to pull her against him, to feel her soft body against his, but he didn't have the strength. But when she snuggled against him, resting her head on his shoulder, he wrapped his arm around her, pressing a kiss to the top of her head.

"That was...*amazing*!" she whispered to him.

Rayed might have nodded, but he wasn't sure about anything at the moment. Except for the fact that she'd just sealed her fate. Emma was his woman now!

Chapter 7

Emma stepped hesitantly out of the bedroom, wearing a new pair of wool slacks and the softest silk blouse she'd ever felt. New underwear too and make up that was *so* expensive, she felt strange even touching it. A staff member had procured these items for her and they'd magically appeared in the bedroom while she'd showered this morning.

Smoothing nervous hands down her hips, she looked around, trying to figure out where to go within this monstrously huge house.

Thankfully, the hallway opened up to an open walkway that looked down onto the great room below. There was a large, U shaped sofa with a massive coffee table in the middle, an enormous window that looked out at the city's skyline and a large, polished table with places for eight people.

Unfortunately, knowing the layout didn't tell her much about where she was in regards to the city. Looking out at the large windows, she could see the skyline of Philadelphia, but Emma wasn't someone who could look at the buildings in the distance and know if she was north, south, east, or west of her apartment.

Nor did she have any clue how to get back to her apartment.

Thankfully, she spotted Rayed easily enough since he was sitting at the head of the dining room table, surrounded by papers and files. There was also another man standing off to the side, handing him more papers that Rayed needed to sign. The man spoke softly as he explained, but Rayed still reviewed each document before signing, although there was no way he could read everything in the quick sweep of his eyes over the papers.

Emma must have made a sound, because Rayed looked up and spotted her, said something to the other man, and stood up, coming to greet her as she nervously walked down the stairs.

"Good morning," he grumbled in that low, husky voice when she reached the bottom stair. "How are you feeling this morning?"

Emma blushed, thinking of all of the demands she'd screamed earlier. "I'm fine," she replied. Not wanting him to know how shy she felt at this moment, she forced her smile to widen and added, "Better than fine, actually."

He laughed softly, his hand reaching up to push her hair back. One finger slid along her forehead just underneath the knot on her forehead. "Are you still in pain?"

She lifted her hand as well, barely touching the spot. "I would have thought that I would be in pain, but I'm not." She shrugged. "I guess I just have a hard head."

He lifted a dark eyebrow at that, then took her hand and led her over to the table. "What would you like for lunch?"

"Lunch?" she gasped, looking around. Sure enough, the angle of the sun was well over the top of the house with very few shadows.

"Yes, lunch. I'm afraid I kept you in bed for far too long this morning."

Emma opened her mouth to tell him that she didn't mind, but the stranger who had been feeding Rayed papers moments ago stepped forward to hand Rayed a cell phone. "Governor Mitchell is on the line for you, Your Highness," the man murmured, then stepped back.

"This might be the phone call that you've been waiting for," Rayed told her, then pressed a button and greeted the pompous governor. "Good morning, Governor Mitchell," he started off. "I apologize for our canceled breakfast meeting. Something came up that had to be dealt with immediately." He glanced over at Emma, chuckling softly when she blushed. Both of them knew exactly what had "come up".

The conversation was brief and mostly one sided, with Rayed agreeing every few moments. Then the call ended and Rayed handed the phone back to his assistant. "He wants to meet me for dinner tonight to discuss a business opportunity. He mentioned that he got another large investor last night, so there's room for just one more person. He wants to speak with me."

Emma's curiosity was instantly piqued. "Do you know what this mysterious opportunity is about?" she asked, smiling as he wrapped an arm around her waist and pulled her against him. Gripping his arms, she let her hands slide higher so they rested on his shoulders. Goodness, she loved his shoulders!

"No idea, but I'm hoping that you'll accompany me so that we can find out together."

She grinned, then lifted onto her toes to kiss him. "Thank you!" she whispered.

"How is your shoulder and wrist?"

"Both are just a dull throb at the moment, but I took some more acetaminophen, so hopefully even that will die away."

"Good. Are you hungry?"

She laughed. "After this morning? I'm starving!"

Rayed pulled out a chair and she carefully sat down, not entirely sure what to do. Men never, ever, pulled out her chair to help her sit down. It was such an old fashioned custom, but as he scooted the chair in for her, Emma found the gesture charming.

"Are you lying about your pain level?" he asked as he resumed his seat at the head of the table.

She grinned, resting her injured wrist on her lap. "Not a chance. I'm a certifiable pain-wimp. I don't like pain on any level, so if my head starts throbbing, I'll let you know at once."

"Good." A servant appeared and smiled expectantly at them. "Now what would you like for breakfast or lunch?"

Emma blinked, not sure what he meant. "I'm sorry, but what do you mean?"

Rayed lifted a dark eyebrow. "It's a simple question. Are you sure you're feeling better?"

She hmphed a bit and her amused glare turned to a glowering one. "I'll just have whatever is on the menu," she told him.

He chuckled. "Emma, we're not in a hotel. I've rented this house because I have a great deal of business here in the city." He nodded towards the servant. "Now if you tell him what you'd like to eat, we could get on with figuring our strategy for tonight."

Still, Emma hesitated, not wanting to be a burden.

Thankfully, Rayed understood her hesitation and said to the servant, "We'll have eggs benedict with fruit on the side, thank you."

The man nodded, bowed, and hurried from room.

"Eggs benedict?" she whispered. "Isn't that hard to make?"

"Not for a chef," he replied, then leaned forward and slid a tablet across the table. "Read this."

Emma looked down, not sure what to brace herself for this time. But as she read the headlines, she gasped, then anger surged through her. "How could he?" she hissed. "What was he thinking? This can't possibly work! People will be furious and..." She froze, lifting her eyes from the report about Governor Mitchell. "He didn't!" she whispered, the headline making her feel sick.

"He did," Rayed confirmed with a short nod.

"But...why? This isn't even a problem! Why would he suggest a new sales tax just so that he can pay to install thirty foot fencing around all of the city's playgrounds?" She glanced down at the article, scanning the words. "Has there been an increase in child abduction cases within the state?"

Rayed shrugged. "Good question."

"I don't understand this," she grumbled.

"Don't you?" he prompted.

The servant returned with two plates. He set them in front of Rayed and Emma and she stared down at the most beautiful set of eggs benedict she'd ever seen. Even the fruit was cut in a lovely rose shape! "Good grief!" she whispered, then lifted her eyes to Rayed. "Didn't we just request this meal a minute ago?"

He merely smiled as he pulled the linen napkin down over his lap. "It probably tastes even better than it looks. The chef I hired for my time here is excellent. He's a graduate of the Culinary Institute of America and has worked at some of the most creative restaurants in the country."

Emma picked up her knife and fork, and stared down at the meal. "I can't cut into this," she whispered to him, not wanting the servants to hear her.

"Why not?" he asked, mercilessly slicing into the eggs so that the soft yolk slowly spread over the ham and toasted English muffin.

"Because it's too beautiful!" she told him with a tone that implied that he should have understood that already.

He merely chuckled and pointed to her plate with his fork. "Dig in. The chef would be insulted if you didn't eat it simply because it was too pretty."

She glanced down at her plate again, then groaned as she sliced into the food. She was actually starving, having missed dinner last night because of her tumble down the stairs and...!

"Dragon!" she whispered, looking up at Rayed.

His hand froze halfway to his mouth as he frowned at her curiously. "Dragon?"

She nodded forcefully and put her cutlery down. "Yes. I had a nightmare the night before last that featured a dragon coming to torment me." She bit her lip, trying to remember the dream, but the images were still just flutters through her mind. "I didn't think anything of it yesterday morning. But last night, I saw the dragon again. I think it was a tattoo on someone's arm!" She concentrated and nodded her head.

Emma clutched at her linen napkin, then extended her unwounded hand towards him on the table. "Yes! Last night when I was in the emergency department, I kept trying to remember something and I knew that there was a detail that I had to tell you. The pain in my head was too intense to think and then the meds kicked in and..." she sighed, rubbing her forehead again as the throbbing increased. Concentration was still a struggle.

"Your head is aching again, isn't it?" he demanded.

Emma slowly...carefully...turned her head to find him kneeling beside her chair, concern in his dark, wonderful eyes.

She tried to speak, but the pain was too intense. She paused for a moment, then started again. This time, she was successful. "Yes, but I can't..." she paused, forcing herself to relax as the pain became overwhelming. "Just give me a moment."

"Stop trying to force it, Emma," he encouraged, standing up and kissing her shoulder. "Just relax and it will come to you."

She nodded and relaxed. He was right and as soon as she stopped trying to remember, the tension in the back of her neck eased up and the throbbing slowly ebbed to bearable levels. With relief, she smiled to Rayed. "I'm fine now," she assured him.

He returned to his chair, but Emma saw the continued concern in his eyes and her heart warmed. It had been a long time since anyone other than Amanda had shown anything beyond than mild lust for her, and none of the men in her past had ever cared if she was in pain. The men she'd dated in the past certainly hadn't cared much about her well-being, other than to try and get her to go to bed with them.

In an effort to ease his concern, she picked up her knife and fork, slicing off a bite of the eggs even though her stomach wasn't quite ready for food. And yet, the moment she popped the creamy eggs covered in tangy hollandaise sauce into her mouth, her eyes widened with surprise. "Oh my! This is delicious!" And took another bite. Then another! Thankfully, the food seemed to actually ease the nausea. Apparently, she'd become too hungry. The food must be helping more than she realized because the throbbing in her head eased a bit more. Emma didn't delude herself into thinking that she was fully recovered. No, the dull throbbing in her head and the twinge in her shoulder and wrist reminded her that she wasn't going to recover immediately from last night's tumble.

And that realization only irritated her more! Someone had pushed her down the stairs! Someone...with a dragon tattoo! Had she seen someone with that tattoo last night? Not including the arm that pushed her down the stairs.

No, she couldn't remember seeing anyone with a distinctive tattoo milling among the elite members of the wealthy society last night.

She'd ponder that factoid later. Right now, she needed to concentrate on the day ahead of her.

"So, you'll come to dinner with me?"

She grinned at him as she bit into a piece of watermelon. "I wouldn't miss it for the world. I'm eager to find out why the governor needed to distract the world with the threat of thirty foot high fencing. What could he actually be doing?"

"I'll need to change clothes before we meet Governor Mitchell for dinner tonight." She gestured to her slacks and silk blouse. "This is too elegant for my bimbo persona."

Rayed allowed his eyes to move down her figure, his skin heating up at just the suggestion of what he now knew was underneath the soft silk blouse.

"I think you look lovely, but I'd never argue with a woman who wants to expose more skin in my presence."

She laughed, then cringed slightly as the throbbing increased. Thankfully, it eased quickly. "No laughing," she chided him as she stood up. She definitely needed more painkillers, but she'd choose the milder kind over the prescription the doctor had written for her. The acetaminophen worked extremely well and didn't muddle her mind. "Where are the kitchens?" she asked, turning slowly to look for the mysterious doorway that might lead to the kitchen.

"What for?" Rayed asked, sliding a hand down her back. He couldn't seem to stop touching her, even if it was just with his eyes. But as his hand moved over her silk-covered back, he knew that it was more than just needing to touch her. And it wasn't just sex either. Rayed wanted a hell of a lot more than just sex.

Emma shifted slightly, turning to touch his arm. "I wanted to thank the chef for the excellent breakfast."

Rayed took her hand, lacing his fingers through hers. "No need. I pay the man extremely well."

Emma followed Rayed, but he could tell that she was hesitant. Another point in her favor. The woman was too sweet and kind, he thought. But that was okay. He'd protect her from the viciousness of palace life.

Several hours later, Rayed was gritting his teeth in an effort to stop himself from tossing Emma over his shoulder and hauling her out of the restaurant.

"This is nice," she replied, looking around as they walked through the elegant restaurant decorated in an old-world Italian style. The hostess led them out to the terrace where the late evening sunshine sparkled through the trees. Large, maroon umbrellas shaded the tables and there was a soft breeze drifting through the tables.

"Lovely, but keep your wits about you," Rayed replied, tucking her hand onto his elbow. "Something isn't right." He paused, turned to the guards that were following and whispered something to one of them. The guard nodded, then backed up and started muttering in the microphone hidden at his wrist.

"Your instincts kicking in?" she asked, looking around mildly, pretending to be bored by the elegant décor.

"Something like that," he replied.

The hostess led them to a private dining room. The governor and a woman that Rayed suspected to be his wife were already in the room. The couple turned and the governor's entire face lit up with eagerness.

"Your Highness!" the short, slightly rotund man called out, shifting his glass of bourbon to his other hand. "I'm thrilled that you were able to fit us into your busy schedule on such short notice." He shook Rayed's hand, completely ignored Emma, then turned and gestured to the older woman. "This is my wife, Doris Mitchell. When she heard I was dining with you tonight, she insisted on accompanying me. I hope you don't mind?"

Emma giggled, leaned against Rayed, and smiled vapidly at the other woman.

"I don't mind at all," Rayed replied, wrapping an arm around Emma's waist as he tried to hide his amusement. She'd slipped easily into the bimbo persona and he had to admit that it was a fascinating transition. "Mrs. Mitchell, it is a pleasure to meet you." He lifted her hand to his lips, kissing her knuckles in an effort to impress the woman. He wanted the governor and his wife completely oblivious to Emma's, and his, real mission.

The thought caught him off-guard. When had Emma's goal become his as well? When had he decided to join forces with her versus simply allowing her to tag along and do her thing?

He didn't know, but it might have been some time last night when she'd snuggled into his arms, sighing with pleasure.

Yeah, that had to be it, he told himself.

And yet, he knew it was a much deeper connection than just physical. They were connected. He'd known it practically from the first moment she'd tripped in her glorious red dress.

"So, how about a cocktail before we sit down to dinner?" the governor suggested, lifting his hand in the air. Immediately, a waiter stepped forward and bowed ever so slightly. "Get these fine people a drink, my good man!" the governor urged, his voice shifting to include a slight, southern twang.

The waiter turned to Rayed. "What can I get you?"

Rayed considered his options, then decided to just throw himself into the role. "I'll have a glass of wine. A rosé."

Emma giggled and Rayed looked at her intently. She giggled again, leaned her head against his shoulder and batted her long lashes as she asked, "Can I have a lemon drop martini?"

The waiter bowed and turned to leave, but Rayed hadn't been watching the waiter. He'd been looking at Governor Mitchell and caught the barely concealed sneer, as well as the lustful gaze a moment later. That was odd, Rayed thought. He'd heard the whispers that the governor was gay. So why would he be lusting after Emma? Maybe bisexual? Or was the governor's lust directed at him? Rayed considered that possibility for a moment, but then he was distracted by Emma's soft breast against his arm.

Doris must have noticed as well, because she put a hand on Emma's arm, distracting everyone. "Dear, would you mind telling me where you bought this adorable dress?" She laughed lightly, guiding Emma to the far side of the room. "It's fascinating how courageous you are to wear something like this! You have such a confidence about you."

Emma giggled again and Rayed almost laughed out loud. Emma wore a skintight dress that teetered on the edge of inappropriate. She was, again, in four inch high heels and she teetered about, trying to appear frail and defenseless. He heard something along the lines of "The most adorable little store over on the waterfront..." but Doris guided Emma out of earshot.

Rayed knew exactly what was going on and also knew what Emma would need for her "big reveal". So, he slapped a hand to his chest, acting as if his cell phone was vibrating, then said, "I'm so sorry, Governor, but I really must take this call. If it's who I think it is, I'll need to just make a comment, then I can put the phone away for dinner."

"Of course!" Kevin replied and even moved away, standing with his back against the wall as he pretended to wait patiently for Rayed to finish the call.

Rayed walked several paces away, speaking quickly in Arabic. There wasn't anyone on the phone. He was actually speaking to one of his bodyguards, explaining that he needed to move close enough so that the governor's entire conversation could be recorded. He knew it was doable with the communications systems that his guards wore at all times. It was necessary for any sort of investigation after a meeting. And recordings were especially important in the case of an assassination attempt. Any kind of sound was recorded for future analysis and investigation, if needed.

The guard immediately understood, silently nodding his understanding and acceptance. Rayed, "finished" his call and pretended to hang up, then handed his phone to the guard who made a show of pocketing it.

"There!" Rayed replied, returning to the governor. The man primped a bit, smoothing a strand of hair and...damn, but the entire top of the guy's head shifted slightly as well. He was wearing a toupee? Even more fascinating.

"So, what did you want to talk to me about?" Rayed asked, wanting to get this conversation over with so that he could enjoy the entertainment.

Mitchell hesitated, pausing for effect as his lips curled up slightly. "Internet," he finally explained.

Rayed's eyebrows lifted. "You don't have adequate internet service to cover the entire state yet?" he asked, even though he knew the answer. He glanced over at Emma, wondering what Doris was saying to keep her out of the way.

"Of course the entire state has internet," the governor replied with a hearty guffaw. "But why not offer certain areas *cheaper* internet?"

Rayed was starting to understand where this "investment" was heading. "Perhaps because one doesn't make as much of a profit when the internet fees are too low?" Rayed offered. If he was right, this wasn't going to be good for the voters. It wasn't going to be good for anyone beyond the investors in this company.

Kevin shifted, his back to the ladies now. Rayed knew that this was when he'd hear the crux of the business opportunity.

"Here's what we're trying to do." He glanced around and hesitated when one of the guards inched closer.

"Don't worry about him," Rayed assured the governor. "He's just a nervous nelly. You're closer than he prefers, so he gets closer to stop you from hurting me."

Kevin laughed uproariously, as if what Rayed had just said was hilarious. Rayed kept his expression neutral as he waited for the laughter to ease up.

When Kevin settled again, he continued in a more serious tone. "Yeah, everyone has internet. And in most areas, it's pretty good." He moved closer, then stopped when Rayed's guards moved in, looking grim and determined. Kevin chuckled, then stepped back, but leaned forward as if trying to convey a secret. "Here's what we're going to do. I have a contact with a special internet provider who stealthily moves into an area that is already serviced by one of the larger providers. This company has new technology that causes sporadic interruption of service with the other companies. The customers in that area eventually get sick of the bad service and intermittent interruptions."

He shifted again, trying to convey a stronger connection than was real as Rayed gave his guard the inconspicuous hand signal to hold off. The guard immediately froze, but Rayed knew that the recording was in operation. "Once everyone is really pissed off, my guy will go into the neighborhood and offer discounts to anyone willing to sign up with his company. The other internet operators will move out of the area because it's just too expensive to operate. They'll shift their internet equipment to more profitable areas. Once he's the only operator in the neighborhood, BAM!" Rayed jerked back slightly while Kevin chuckled. "We stick the customers with a huge price increase." Kevin pulled back, lifted his glass to his mouth and practically poured his bourbon down his throat. After swallowing, he shrugged, a triumphant grin on his chubby features. "By that point, there's no alternative. We're in and no one has any other option but to continue to pay our prices."

Rayed finally understood. Everything inside of him rebelled at the corruption this man was implementing. It was pure market manipulation and it was illegal on so many levels.

Thankfully, Rayed kept his revulsion well hidden. "How is this company going to move in so easily?"

Kevin lifted his hands in the air by his sides. "That's the beauty of this whole plan! I'm the one who appoints the board members. And the senators in the state legislature, most of which are in my party and are the current majority, approve my appointees. My party rubber-stamps every candidate I nominate. So the company has pretty much carte blanche to move in and set up their equipment. Once everyone in the area has shifted over to this new service, the board of directors will approve the price increase and no one can fight them." He chuckled and waved Rayed over to the bar. With a nod, Kevin dismissed the bartender. "It's a sure thing." He reached behind the bar to pour himself more bourbon, then glanced at Rayed's wine glass, which was still full. Kevin barely suppressed a sneer at the feminine alcohol. After refilling his glass, he took a hefty swallow and continued. "With my nominations and my senators rubber stamping my nominees, we can get several neighborhoods on board with this new internet company quickly and without any negative publicity. Plus, I can pass laws and reforms that will make life difficult for the old internet players, forcing them to concentrate their efforts elsewhere."

"What about lawsuits?"

Kevin laughed and waved his glass of bourbon dismissively. "All taken care of. The neighborhoods we've chosen are low income areas.

The residents don't have the wherewithal to file lawsuits. They just have to accept what they get. Hell, these people don't even research what a reasonable price for internet services is, so whatever we offer them, they're happy to pay it. And besides, I have a tech team in place that can set up websites and blog sites that praise this company. If anyone actually goes online to research prices, my team will have websites ready with answers to those questions. They'll just ramp up the price so that everything these people see online confirms that the price they are paying is reasonable and fair." Kevin laughed again, shaking his head. "We only move into the low income areas. Those communities usually work two jobs, just to make ends meet. So they are too busy to question anything."

"What if someone gets wind of what you are doing?" Rayed asked, gripping his glass of wine tightly to stop himself from punching the ass in the nose. He was about as corrupt as one could be!

"If anyone raises an alarm, then I just toss out some crazy legislation, some random headline, that preys on the fears of parents and how something or someone could hurt their kids. Parenting fear is a powerful distraction! That way, everyone starts worrying about that issue and they forget about the whispers regarding higher internet prices." He chuckled softly. "Didn't you see the headline this morning about fencing playgrounds?"

Rayed focused on keeping his tone neutral. "Yeah, I saw something about that this morning. Is there a significant number of child abductions on playgrounds recently?"

Kevin rolled his eyes. "Hell no! In fact, just the opposite. Child abductions are actually down in most areas. The police have been quite effective lately. But the parents don't know that." He sighed, shaking his head. "I can create any headline that 'protects' children and parents go wild! All the news has to report is the latest fear and the parents go crazy. It's like a magic wand, hiding anything I want while I distract the public."

"Sounds like you've got this all figured out."

"I do!" Kevin assured him. "This is a sure thing." Kevin paused and looked around, watching the ladies who were still chatting across the room for a moment. "Why don't you think about it for a day or two. But no longer. I need to finalize the investors by Friday. If you want in, I can help you be a part of this operation."

Rayed nodded, but didn't commit to anything. "Thanks for the few days. It will give me a bit of time to consider." He clinked his glass against Kevin's, suppressing his laugh when the man failed to hide his sneer at the glass of wine. Obviously, Kevin didn't think that wine, much less rosé wine, was a manly drink.

"Good enough," Kevin replied, then turned to glance at his wife and Emma. "Should we order dinner? This place has some excellent options. I want to try the steak. I've heard it's amazing!"

Kevin turned and glanced at his wife, who immediately led Emma back to the center of the room where the table had been set up. Emma glanced up at Rayed, but quickly looked away. She was trying very hard to hide her own laughter, but Rayed also saw the fatigue in her eyes. She was exhausted and probably in pain, he thought. But she wasn't willing to let go of this story. Fortunately, he could finally tell her exactly what was going on so she could investigate. Now that they knew what was happening, he could even help her with his own investigators.

The rest of the evening was uneventful, especially compared to the revelations during the cocktail hour. It still took them several hours to get through the meal. Rayed watched Emma carefully and saw the strain around her eyes intensify. She was about ready to fall over, he thought. So when Kevin and Doris suggested dessert, Rayed shook his head.

"We need to pass on dessert, but I appreciate the invitation to dine with you tonight," he said. Normally, he would simply pay for the entire meal, even though the governor had invited him and Emma. But tonight, revulsion at the governor's machinations were still angering him, so he didn't bother. This guy was completely corrupt. He would probably add this meal as a deduction to his taxes and use it as a write off. But if anyone asked, Rayed would be sure to tell them that it was a completely social evening. If they could gather enough evidence, then the governor wouldn't stand a chance!

Leaving the dining room, he wanted to scoop Emma up into his arms, and carry her out to the car, hoping that would somehow ease her pain. But she stayed ramrod straight as they made their way through the main dining room. He had to give her credit though. If he hadn't known her so well, he wouldn't have suspected that she was in pain. Other than a slight tightening of the muscles around her eyes, Emma had remained in character all night, offering inane comments that had nothing to do with the current topic of conversation.

She was a real trooper, he thought admiringly.

"Let's get you back to my place and into bed," he suggested and, since they were out on the sidewalk now, he picked her up. Emma melted in his arms, resting her aching head against his shoulder. He didn't bother putting on a seat belt this time. He merely held her in his lap as his guards drove through the late night traffic back to the house.

Chapter 8

Emma had a sense of déjà vu. Opening her eyes, she stared at the teal colored ceiling, trying to make sense of the night before. And just like yesterday morning, a heavy hand was draped over her waist. It took her several moments to realize where she was and how she'd gotten here. But as soon as the memories returned, she smiled and rolled over.

Rayed was still asleep, his long, dark lashes fanned out against his tanned skin. For a moment, she just stared at him, taking in the amazing sense of his power and the way he made her feel. He was such a large man, both in personality as well as just sheer physical size. Well over six feet and packed with delicious muscles.

He hadn't made love to her last night, probably because she'd been too exhausted to deal with any sort of physical interaction. The pain reliever had worn off too early. She really should have remembered to keep extra painkillers in her purse. Rayed reminded her to take some pain medicine before falling asleep. All Emma had wanted to do was strip off the uncomfortable clothes and crawl into bed until the pain went away, or sleep took over. He'd stopped her, insisting that she take the meds. Then he'd tucked her under the cool sheets, kissed her forehead and...held her until she'd fallen asleep.

"You're staring at me," he groused with his eyes still closed.

She laughed softly, her fingers tracing his muscles. "And you're not asleep, like I thought you were."

"I woke up as soon as you moved."

"So, you were just faking it?"

His eyes popped open and he looked at her. "I'd never fake it with you, Emma."

Her teasing smile faded at the sincerity in his tone. Leaning forward, she kissed him gently to show how much she appreciated his vow of honesty. "Thank you for taking care of me last night," she whispered.

"Thank you for caring enough to put yourself out there for people you don't even know," he replied, then pulled her up until she was draped on top of him.

"You're naked," she gasped, shifting her body against his.

"So are you," he countered.

Emma might have laughed if she wasn't so turned on. That lust ramped up higher still when his strong hands moved up her ribcage until he was cupping her breasts. "You have something else on your mind this morning." She laughed when he chuckled.

"And your powers of observation are just as sharp as ever." He froze, his eyes moving away from her breasts to look into her eyes. "How is your head?"

She paused, surprised to notice her head didn't ache this morning. "It's actually pretty good." And with that, she shifted against him, her body hot and wet, more than ready to take him into hers. But he pulled back and she groaned. With a muttered curse, she reached over and, from last night's experience, Emma knew that there was a box of condoms in the bedside table. "I really need to get on birth control," she muttered as she ripped open the condom.

He held her still for a moment and Emma pulled her concentration away from the protection she was trying to unwrap.

"Does that mean that you're thinking of this relationship in a more long term manner?" he asked, his voice heavy with meaning.

Emma froze, her heart pounding, but for a different reason now. "I didn't mean...you don't have to...I just...I wanted...!"

Interrupting her stammering, he tightened his grip on her waist. "I want longer, Emma," he told her.

Emma's heart thudded harder. "You...do?"

"Hell yes!" he said, then grabbed the condom. He rolled it quickly down his shaft. When it was in place, he took hold of her waist and rolled their bodies until he was on top. "What do *you* want?" he asked, but didn't give her a chance to reply since he was already sliding into her wet heat.

Emma wanted to scream to him that she wanted him. Forever. But that wasn't what she wanted, was it? And if she actually admitted that it was what she wanted, would he leave? Men didn't like women who wanted commitment. So instead of replying, she closed her eyes end let him take control. She wrapped her legs around his waist and slid her hands around his neck, letting her fingers dig into his wonderful, amazing shoulders. Her voice might be silent about her hopes and dreams for their future. But her body screamed that she loved him.

And as she reached that beautiful pinnacle, Emma cried out, her head thrown back as she tightened her grip around Rayed, thrilling with every thrust as the pleasure increased until she thought she might actually pass out.

She was almost relieved when she heard Rayed's groan as he reached his own fulfillment, and then she was tumbled backwards, the sheets and blankets surrounding them as he cradled her gently against his chest.

Still intimately connected to her, Rayed gazed at the woman who had so completely captured his heart. Was this love? He suspected that his feelings had developed well beyond lust. But could love happen in just three days? It seemed impossible to be in love in such a short period of time.

No, this was merely lust and dopamine. It was the passion of a new relationship. It was...hell, he didn't want to let her go!

"How is your head?" he asked, gently brushing a stray lock of dark hair out of her eyes. He loved her eyes. The bright blue of her eyes was like looking through a window into her soul. Hadn't some poet said that? Shakespeare? Or someone else? He didn't know, but it was one of the most accurate statements he'd ever read. Because he could see the slight pain in the tension around her eyes, and yet, she was beaming up at him as if nothing was wrong with the world.

"My head is fine." Her legs shifted, the soft skin of her inner thighs caressing him.

"You're lying," he argued and pulled out of her. She gasped, and he kissed her lightly before grabbing a tissue and taking care of the condom before he flicked the sheet back over her. "Stay put for a moment. I'll get you some pain pills."

He heard her sigh as he moved across the room to the bathroom. Grabbing a couple of pain relievers and a cup of water, he paused to stare at himself in the mirror. Was that a smile on his face? What the hell? He never smiled! Or he hadn't smiled in a while. Ever since Lila had come into Tazir's life, he thought.

That only reinforced his decision to somehow convince Emma to come to Fahre with him.

Turning, he cradled the pills in his hand as he strolled back to the bedroom. Now he just had to convince her that they could make it together.

Chapter 9

"What's on the agenda today?" he asked an hour later as they strolled down the stairs, hand in hand.

"Today," she asserted firmly, "you are going to do whatever it is that you do. And I'm going to work on my own."

He shook his head as he pulled the dining room chair out for her. "My schedule is fluid."

Emma admired the man as he sat down at the head of the table. As soon as his voice was heard, his aide, a short, efficient man, had appeared at his elbow. She hadn't explored the house because during the time she spent with Rayed, they'd either been in that bedroom or here at the table eating the delicious food.

"What would you like for breakfast this morning?" he asked her as another servant appeared.

Emma bit her lip, not sure she wanted anything. "I'll just have coffee," she told the waiter.

"And fruit," Rayed interjected, looking up from whatever was on the tablet his aide had handed him.

"I'm not very hungry. Last night's dinner was *very* rich."

Her lips twitched in amusement at the irritated expression in Rayed's eyes. But it was concern, she reminded herself.

She placed a gentle hand on his as she said, "I assure you, I know how to get food if I get hungry, Rayed. I'm old enough to know how to cook food myself." She tilted her head the side, unaware of how her eyes sparkled teasingly. "And I'm even capable of driving to the grocery store to get something, if I want it."

He glared at her for another long moment, but in the end, he nodded to the waiter. "I'll have my usual," he requested.

He finished reading whatever information was on the tablet, gave instructions to his aide in what Emma suspected was Arabic, and then they were left alone.

"What's your regular breakfast?" she asked.

"A vegetable omelet with fruit on the side," he explained. "What are we doing today?"

Emma paused and smiled at the waiter as he poured coffee for them into delicate porcelain cups, then set the coffee pot on the table and disappeared. Emma wondered how often they would be interrupted during the meal, but kept her complaints to herself.

When they were alone again, she continued. "I am going to do some research on the various internet companies, especially a couple that the governor mentioned last night. I'm going to find out when they started doing business, what technology they use as opposed to the other companies, the prices they offer right now versus the rates they charge in other areas and chart the pricing over time." She took a sip of her coffee. "And you," she asserted firmly, "are going to work on whatever it was that your personal assistant needs you to review and upon which, decisions are waiting."

He chuckled, sipping his coffee during her explanation. "Fine. You do your research, but I'll get you set up here with a computer and–"

Emma lifted a hand, interrupting his planning. "I have my own computer and research notes at my apartment. I'll work there."

He was shaking his head before she could finish. "You can't work at your apartment, Emma," he sighed. He lifted his hand and murmured something to one of the guards that Emma hadn't noticed a moment ago. The guard immediately nodded and disappeared.

"What did you say to him?"

"He's retrieving the note that your roommate informed us about yesterday." The guard returned and laid a plastic covered piece of paper on the table, then went back to whatever hiding place he'd been in before.

"This note...?" she leaned forward, reading the words with horror as her stomach gave a sickening lurch. "Where did this come from?"

"Amanda found it underneath your apartment door yesterday morning."

Emma's mouth fell open. "Is she...?"

"She's fine. She wasn't hurt, just a bit nervous. And angry," Rayed added with a slight smile.

Emma started to stand up, but Rayed put a hand to her arm. "She's fine, Emma. I had a guard stay with her last night. Nothing happened. I'm rotating body guards during the day to ensure her safety. She is perfectly safe, so you should feel free to continue your investigation."

Emma stared deeply into his eyes, trying to determine if he was telling the truth or holding out on her. "Why didn't you tell me about this note when it arrived? If she found it yesterday, I should have been told immediately."

One side of his mouth quirked upwards before he said, "Apparently, your roommate doesn't go out every day. So she hadn't entered the foyer until then." He tilted his head slightly. "How is that possible?"

Emma rubbed her suddenly throbbing head as worry washed over her. "Amanda is a mystery writer. She works out of our apartment and only leaves when she needs to go to the library or hit the grocery store."

"That would explain why she didn't notice it before now."

Emma pulled her eyes away from Rayed and read the note again. *"The fall down the stairs was just a warning. Stop and you won't be hurt worse."*

"Stop? Stop what? Until last night, I didn't even know what was going on!"

Rayed leaned back as a beautiful omelet filled with onions, red peppers, green onions, zucchini and some other vegetables was set in front of him. A plate was put in front of her as well. She stared down at the decorative fruit in stunned silence. This morning, the fruit wasn't cut in the shape of flowers, but the cantaloupe and honeydew melon was still presented in an artistic manner. Emma couldn't help but be impressed once again with the chef's eye for detail. Everything looked exquisite. If Emma weren't still so full from the pasta meal she'd eaten last night, she'd be tempted to ask for something more, just to see how the chef presented it.

"This looks beautiful," she sighed, unconsciously rubbing her forehead. "So does your omelet."

"Do you want some?" he asked, his knife and fork poised above the meal.

"No, thank you," she replied softly, then frowned down at the note again. "Are you sure that Amanda is okay?"

He took a bite and chewed, nodding his head. "Absolutely. Your friend is safe. If there is any concern that she might not be, my guards have instructions to take her to a safe house." He lifted a hand to stop her next question. "My guards tried to convince her to go to a safe house already, but Amanda refused. She wasn't angry," he continued, a strange expression marring his handsome features. "Just...incredibly polite."

Emma smiled slightly and nodded. "Yeah, that sounds like Amanda." She lifted her eyes again. "Are your guards okay?"

He stopped the bite that he'd been bringing to his mouth and looked over at her again. "Are my guards okay?" he repeated, confusion in his tone. "Why wouldn't they be okay?"

Emma chuckled softly. "Because Amanda can be...headstrong." Her grin widened. "In a very polite way."

He grunted, then shrugged. "My guards are even more so." Then he pointed to the note with his fork. "What do you think that's about?" He cut another portion of his omelet. "Besides the obvious, of course."

"You don't think it's merely about someone wanting me to stop investigating whatever the governor is doing?"

He shook his head as he took a large swallow of coffee. "As far as my guards can ascertain, no one knows what you're doing, and the governor is oblivious. Which means they aren't aware of your official investigation." He nodded towards the note. "So if they don't know that we're looking into the governor's corruption with the internet company, and since we'd just figured out what was happening last night, then they think you're doing something else. The real question to ask; what do they want you to stop doing?"

She stared at him for a long moment, trying to think back. Her head was aching, but it wasn't painful enough to stop her from concentrating, thank goodness.

When she thought back to the previous few nights, she realized she hadn't really been doing any investigating. "My only suspicion was that the governor's crazy headlines were hiding something that he was doing behind the scenes. Now we know that's true, and that he's putting a board of directors in place that will rubber stamp the internet company's ingress to low income neighborhoods, then..."

"But, we still don't know the name of the internet company," Rayed pointed out.

Emma nodded, leaning forward so that her forearms were resting on the table's polished surface. Her fingers wrapped around the steaming cup of coffee as she contemplated the problem. "You're right. Before I figure out who is moving into the neighborhoods, I'll need to figure out who the who is."

He paused in his eating, blinking at her statement. Emma laughed and waved her hand. "I know, that's a convoluted way of saying that we need to figure out who the main company is that wants to move into the area and beat out the competition."

"That should be easy enough to do," he replied, around the last bite of his eggs and vegetables. "If an internet company is currently poised to move into certain low income neighborhoods, their towers should already be built, equipment in place and ready to go. That means that there should be a county record of work permits. We just eliminate the permits that apply to residential, renovation, and commercial buildings that applied over the past...," he paused to think for a moment, then continued, "say six months. Once that's narrowed down, we should be able to figure out which internet companies applied for permits."

Emma was impressed and her smile brightened. "That's an excellent idea!" she gasped, eager to get to work now. "I have a friend at the county recorder's office. She can give me a clue about where to start looking."

"Perfect," Rayed announced, wiping his mouth with the linen napkin. He stood up and reached out to take her hand. "Let's do it."

Emma blinked, but automatically reached out to put her hand in his. "You're not going with me to the county administrative offices, Rayed! You have other issues to deal with and I've taken up too much of your time already."

"I am absolutely coming with you, Emma," he replied calmly, unaffected by her adamant tone. "You're not kicking me out of this investigation now." He leaned closer, kissing her lightly on the mouth. "I'm in it, Emma. We're a team."

"Yes, but you're...you!" she replied, her voice taking on a bit of panic. She'd sort of been hoping to have a bit of time away from Rayed. A bit of time to get her head back on track. Because right now, she was pretty sure that she was falling in love with him!

She needed to stop herself, to analyze what she was feeling, and tell her brain, and her heart, to stop falling for him. He didn't live here. He lived thousands of miles away and he'd be leaving the city as soon as he was finished with whatever business he had going on. She didn't like the idea of him leaving her, but she also knew that it was inevitable.

"You don't think I'm capable of reading through county records to help you discover what you're looking for, Emma?" he asked, his voice soft and smooth.

Breathing in a slow, concentrated breath, Emma forced herself to concentrate on the investigation. She could do this. Both of "this". She could figure out what Governor Mitchell was doing and she could survive whatever "this" was that was happening between herself and Rayed. When both were finished, when she'd revealed the corruption to the voters on Mitchell's systematic fleecing of the hard working residents, she'd shift her focus to figuring out how to recover from her love affair with Rayed.

And yes, she suddenly realized that she was madly in love with the man. This wasn't just a crush or an infatuation. This was core deep, abiding love. She doubted that she'd ever feel this way about anyone again in her life. She loved him. She loved him with her whole heart! Never before had she given herself so completely to a man and Emma hadn't even realized she was doing it! How could she have been so blind? Why hadn't she protected her heart more carefully? Everything about the handsome, intelligent, dynamic man was a walking warning that she was going to get hurt.

Rayed had snuck under her defenses. Not just sexually, though, the physical side of their relationship was shockingly hot! Physically, she'd never released her inhibitions like she had with Rayed. He just...when he touched her...there wasn't any room, no time for inhibitions.

He'd also been so kind and sweet, not to mention, generous when she'd been hurt. He had protected her, sheltered her. Not just her, Emma now knew that he was protecting Amanda as well! How...sweet!

Emma looked up to find Rayed watching her with an odd expression in his eyes as he spoke on the phone. Emma wanted to run and hide, to protect herself from the raw need that was in his gaze. But she couldn't move. Something about him...it had been there from the start...he'd captured her. Even at his first approach when she'd literally fallen into his arms, she'd been caught by Rayed's indomitable personality.

Sighing, she tried to push herself to walk away. She needed to brush her teeth and maybe those few moments alone would give her a little breathing room, a bit of space, to analyze what she'd just realized. But she couldn't move. He watched her with those intense, brown eyes and she was trapped!

The call ended and he walked over to her. "You're panicking, aren't you?" he asked softly as his hand cradled her cheek. "You've just realized that this...whatever is happening between us...is more than just a fling, haven't you?'

Emma opened her mouth to speak, but no sound emerged, so she nodded slowly.

"Good," he replied, nodding himself. He kissed her tenderly. The caress was so soft, so gentle, and yet, it touched her all the way down to her soul! It whispered to her heart and made her want to cry!

Instead, she clung to him. She reached out, clenching his shirt in her fists as she whispered, "You terrify me!"

He leaned his forehead against hers. "You terrify *me*, Emma."

He pulled her into his arms, his chin resting lightly against the top of her head as he hugged her tightly. "We'll figure this out together, okay?"

Emma nodded because she still couldn't speak. However, she wasn't sure if he was referring to the investigation or their relationship. What were they going to figure out together? Both? She certainly hoped so! Emma definitely didn't want to be left at the end of this investigation with a broken heart.

But she couldn't really figure out a solution to their relationship. He lived in Fahre. He was freaking prince. No, not just a prince. A crown prince. He was in line to rule the freaking country! She was a lowly investigative reporter with a nose for sniffing out stories.

"Stop it, Emma," he admonished, pulling back slightly so that he could look into her eyes. "Let's do this together and not worry about the future for now. We'll figure it out."

"Yes." She nodded to emphasize her agreement, then had to reach up and wipe an errant tear from her cheek. "Yes. We'll figure this out together."

"Good." He took her hands and kissed her fingertips, then laced his fingers with hers. "We'll start by visiting your friend at the county recorders' office. Baby steps," he told her.

They brushed their teeth and gathered what they'd need for the day. Rayed had already informed his guards of their plans. Yusef had frowned at Rayed with confusion and offered to find the information via their security systems. Fahre had an elaborate computer system with connections to databases all over the world. Anything that their security team didn't have access to, they could hack into with no one ever knowing they were there.

That wasn't anything special. Governments all over the world spied on each other. It wasn't just spying on one's enemies, but on one's allies as well. Every government used whatever methods necessary to gain an advantage.

But Rayed had told him no. "Not yet. This is...," he paused, not sure how to explain. "This is more than just trying to find the records."

He looked at his lead guard and the man nodded, understanding.

Fifteen minutes later, they were heading out the door. Emma was wearing a pair of jeans and a simple tee-shirt while Rayed wore a nice pair of slacks and a tee-shirt that hugged his shoulders and biceps. He looked absolutely delicious and she wondered how she was going to get her head on straight when the man continued to look so distractingly scrumptious!

All day long, they sifted through the records in the administrator's office. But they didn't find anything. They paused around midday for lunch, but went right back to it in the afternoon. By the evening, they still hadn't found anything.

Rayed considered offering his security team's services, but he was enjoying spending time with Emma. They talked and debated during their search. And it was nice to have breakfast, lunch, and dinner with her, even if they hadn't uncovered anything.

That evening, after a delicious dinner with red wine and candlelight, Rayed pulled Emma into his arms and made love to her. It was their first night where it was just the two of them. Emma couldn't get enough of him that night. Since her revelations that morning, her understanding that this time with him was limited, she wanted to absorb as much of him as she could, learn everything he allowed her to know about him.

It was the same over the next five days. The only difference was that Emma refused to let Rayed buy her more clothes. Or more specifically, she refused to allow him to have a mysterious staff member buy her more clothes. She ordered him to take her to her apartment so that she could pack a bag.

Amanda wasn't there, which meant that she was probably at the library working. Amanda forced herself to concentrate when she was building up to the "big reveal" on the who-done-it chapter, the part of her book where she revealed all of the answers to the reader and concluded the story. She tended to hibernate in the library during those times, not logging into the library's internet so that she couldn't distract herself. Distractions meant that she would miss a clue that she needed to tie up, or forgot to explain a part of the mystery. She was very disciplined about her writing methods, unlike several of the other authors Emma knew.

It wasn't until the fifth day of researching that Emma figured out the internet company. It was harder than expected because the company had several different company names. They'd filed permits under ten different shell companies in an effort to hide what they were doing. That was actually pretty smart, she thought as she danced over to where Rayed was sifting through the county database.

"I think I found it!" she whispered.

"You found it?" he asked, swiveling on the hard stool that was set up for just this kind of a search.

"I think so!" she replied, bouncing excitedly on balls of her feet. "Look at this," she said, then spread the printouts she'd accumulated over the past several days. "I know that these records show several different company names. See here?" she pointed to the line at the top. "If you look at the names of the companies, they are all different. Same for their company address. But when I looked into the companies, I found this," she said, spinning her laptop around so that she could show Rayed the link. "This website has the same address as this one," she explained, pointing to one of the permits. "And this one," she said, pointing to another, "is within the same zip code as this one. The addresses are the same on these five permits, but when I looked up the actual address,

I found that it was actually a post office box and that P.O. Box is the same as..." she clicked over to another site, "*this* company, which is also connected to the first one." She flipped back to the previous "company". "Then I went through and checked all of them and..." she pointed to the last four permits. "All four of these permits have different names, but the post office box numbers are located in the same post office!"

He looked at the information, nodding his agreement. "I think you've done it!" he replied and jumped up from his stool, lifting her into his arms for a hug. "You're brilliant!" he said, breathing in the sweet scent of her shampoo. When he pulled back, he said the words he hadn't realized where on the tip of his tongue. "Damn, you are beautiful and brilliant! Marry me!"

Emma pulled back, startled by the unexpected command. "What?"

Rayed groaned, shook his head and forced himself to concentrate on the company. "One thing at a time." He waved his hands slightly, then focused on the records again. "Forget that for now. Let's get back to my place and we'll put all this together."

Emma nodded, but her head was spinning. It took her a moment, but she managed to return her focus to the investigation. "We need to check out Securities and Exchange filings for the parent company. I'm guessing that some of the town council members, the ones that have already approved the various building permits, have bought stock in this parent company. We need to know which members have bought up stock and how much of a stake Governor Mitchell has in the company."

"We should also look up how much money each of these shell companies have donated to his political campaign. If Mitchell was smart, he won't have any stock in the company, but he'll have reaped some financial benefit from this company that is setting up business in the various neighborhoods."

"You're right," Emma replied, biting her lip as her mind flashed back to the "Marry me" command. Focus, she told herself. It was just a joke! A fluke! The man didn't really want to marry her. He'd just said that during a celebratory moment, a moment of triumph!

Pushing the wayward thoughts away, Emma pulled out her phone and called her editor. "I think I've got it," she replied. For the next fifteen minutes, she filled in her boss on what they'd discovered. When her boss told her to write up the story as quickly as possible, Emma grinned confidently. "I'm on it!"

"What did your boss say?"

Emma chuckled. "She said to get a rough draft to her fast!"

He pulled her into his arms. " What do you need to get that done?"

"My laptop and my desk back at my apartment."

"Not a chance," he told her, shaking his head to emphasize his words. "Amanda is safe for now and my guards got wind that the county recorders administrative woman was questioned by a couple of strangers yesterday after we left. Two men were sniffing around, asking why someone was looking through the records." He paused, looking at her carefully. "One of the men had a long, dragon tattoo snaking around his arm."

Emma's eyes widened with that news. She tried to swallow, but her throat was tight as the memories flooded through her.

"A dragon tattoo?"

"Yes. My men are looking for the two men, especially the man with the tattoo. We think that the two men work for either Governor Mitchell or the internet company that is trying to manipulate the state contracts."

Emma nodded, trying to absorb this, trying to put all of the pieces together. She looked down, her mind whirling with that information. But when she looked up at Rayed, she could see more in his eyes.

"What aren't you telling me?" she asked, trying not to panic.

Rayed hesitated, then continued. "Your friend at the county office gave you up, explained that you were a reporter and not some bimbo who didn't know hairspray from perfume. So you're staying with me while you write the story." He kissed her again. "And even after that, until the story is published and the news is out there, you're staying here where I can protect you."

Emma nodded, feeling the tension ease from her shoulders. She hadn't realized how tense she was about this investigation. " I'll take you up on it. The last time I had a sweet story like this, my boss had me writing in the office and sleeping on a cot. Her administrative assistant brought me meals, but everything was takeout. By the time I turned in the story, my blood sodium levels were through the roof from all of the junk food."

He looked at her warily, wrapping his arms around her waist. "You're not going to argue with me?"

She tilted her head further back to smile up at him. "Why would I?" She snuggled closer. "Hanging out with a gorgeous man who feeds me delicious, healthy food? Someone who can fill in the blanks when I forget one of the details we've looked up? I'm all in."

"Excellent," he said, then released her, swatting her bottom as he led her into an office. "Now get to it."

A moment later, she was alone in an elegant office with her laptop and just about every other piece of office equipment she might conceivably need.

For the next twenty-four hours, she typed up what she knew, sleeping only a few hours when she could no longer keep her eyes open. The documents they'd printed out were laid on the floor of the office with only a small pathway from the door to her desk. Every once in a while, Rayed would pop in with another piece of information. Sometimes that new information meant that she needed to revise what she'd already written and other times, the new piece of data merely spurred her fingers to type faster.

There was a sense of urgency now. Emma needed to get this story out to the public, and she knew that her newspaper would also provide the evidence to the department of justice for further investigation. Something this big was going to take down more than one politician. Emma doubted Governor Mitchell would fall. Men like him always landed on their feet. But she could tarnish his reputation a bit. That was her main goal, however, she still wrote the story with him as the pivot around which all the other players revolved. Without Governor Mitchell's efforts, the plan wouldn't have materialized, the internet company wouldn't have had the pull to step in and build their network in the low income neighborhoods, and the price gouging wouldn't be about to take place. Plus, there was a need to stop this company from moving forward to interfere with the service already offered in several other neighborhoods. They'd already infiltrated fifteen areas of the state so far, but there was evidence that they were moving into several more neighborhoods pretty quickly. Soon, without her article to stop them, the company would be the predominant internet provider in the entire state and would have a monopoly. There wouldn't be any way to keep them from raising prices after that.

Two days later, Emma fidgeted on the linen-covered sofa, nibbling at her thumbnail while she waited for Rayed to finish reading her article. He read silently, turning the papers slowly, sometimes going back to re-read something, then moving forward again. Was he confused? Was there some aspect of the investigation, of her article, that didn't flow properly?

She'd let him read the article before her editor, needing his approval more than anyone else. But he was reading so slowly!

Finally, he looked up, carefully setting the article down beside him on the sofa.

"Well?" she asked, jumping up nervously so she could pace. There wasn't enough room in front of the sofa, not with the enormous coffee table in the way. So she walked behind the sofa, still in his line of sight, but with more room to allow her nervous energy to flow.

"It's good," he told her.

"Good?" she whispered. Just good? Her heart sank. It was good. "Good" was a death knell for writers! She'd put her heart and soul into that article. Emma suddenly realized that she'd been *trying* to impress Rayed. She'd wanted him to be wowed by her prose, by the careful way she'd developed the story, and explained all of the details that they'd discovered.

He stood up, resting his fists on his lean hips. "It's amazing, Emma. Truly out...oof!" he grunted when she threw herself into his arms. Laughing, he lifted her up, hugging her as he buried his face in her hair.

She leaned back so she could see into his eyes, needing to know if he was telling the truth. "Really? It's okay? It's better than good?"

"Yes," he said, sliding his hands along her waist. "It's damn incredible."

She grinned, relief rushing through her. "Thank you!"

And with that, she pushed him down onto the sofa, her hands pressing against his shoulders. "I needed to hear that from you," she whispered, and kissed him. For a long moment, she kept kissing him, showing him how much she needed him. Now that the article was finished, she knew that this was the end. Emma needed him to know how much she cared for him, how much she loved him, but she wasn't ready to say the words. She didn't want him to have to deal with the burden of her feelings for him. She had no idea what he'd meant by "more" earlier, but for her, the past ten days had been...heaven!

"So, what is the next step?" he asked her, lacing his fingers behind her back.

"I need to send the story to my editor. But more than that, I need to send her all of the backup for my story." She bit her lower lip. "We still don't know who the guy with the dragon tattoo is." She pulled out another piece of paper. "But I think it's this person." She handed him the report that included a mug shot of a guy with a dragon tattoo curling around his arm. "This man is a hired thug. But I think he's the man who pushed me down the stairs. I don't have any evidence to back up my statement. I don't remember seeing him at any of the events we attended. So maybe I'm wrong."

Rayed looked at the image, then laid the paper down next to him. "I'll have my security team look into the dragon guy. But let's get back to the report for your editor. Why does she need your evidence? Won't she trust you?"

She grinned. "My boss trusts me. But a story this big and potentially catastrophic will need to go through the lawyers first. They'll have to review everything that I've gathered so far, and then connect the dots, just like we did. The bar for news stories of this level is very high. Especially something like this where we're accusing a sitting governor of something so repugnant."

"And illegal. We can't forget that his actions are illegal. He's violated several local, state, and federal laws."

She grimaced. "I also can't forget that the man is a very popular governor. He has a very high approval rating. This story has to be rock solid. I suspect that my editor will even take the story to the district attorney for potential charges."

Rayed nodded. "Things happen a bit differently here in the Unites States."

Emma tilted her head slightly. "What would happen in Fahre?"

He grinned and pulled out of her arms. But not for long. He moved over to the sofa, pulling her down onto his lap. Emma wrapped her arms around his neck, leaning into him. He was an incredibly comfortable "chair".

"In Fahre, if someone came to me with this kind of evidence, I would arrest the politician immediately and send a team of special forces men out to hunt the man with the dragon tattoo. Regarding the politician, we don't have state governors, but we have ten territories. The Territory Minister would be brought up in front of a tribunal. Either Tazir or I would head up that tribunal. We'd hear the evidence and, if we thought the man guilty, he would be stripped of his title and thrown into jail."

"What would happen to his family?"

His mouth twisted at that question. "Well, if there was evidence that the family knew of the minister's illegal activities, they would also be charged. But in most cases, the shame would be enough to force the family members to leave the country. Which is a challenge, since they would probably try to take their ill-gotten money with them. We work with several other countries and sometimes have the power to freeze assets. But sometimes, the families get away with their assets before the minister can stand trial."

"That doesn't seem very fair. I don't like the idea of a wife like Doris living large with the money gotten from something like this."

He shifted, looking down at her. "Are you avoiding the elephant in the room?" he asked.

Emma sighed, hiding her face again his shoulder. "Yes." The answer was barely above a whisper.

"Why?" Rayed asked, rubbing her back soothingly.

"Because I'm afraid."

He kissed the top of her head. "What are you afraid of, *habibi*?"

She turned, looking at him. "Now that the story is written and the mystery solved, I'm afraid that you will have to return to Fahre."

He looked into her blue eyes and sighed. "You're right. I do need to go home. My family needs me."

Emma wanted to scream that she needed him too. She wanted to pound on his chest and tell him that it wasn't fair. She'd finally found someone that she loved, respected, and...and someone who made her feel wonderful. Now he was going to leave her.

"When do you leave?" She buried her face against his neck, not wanting to see his expression as he answered her. Or maybe she didn't want him to see her expression. She closed her eyes tightly, trying to stifle the threatening tears.

"Soon." His thumb stroked her arm. "Will you come with me?"

Emma stilled. Had she heard him correctly? Had he really just asked her to come with him? To be with him longer?

"Emma?" Rayed prompted.

She lifted her head, staring into his eyes. "What do you mean?" She shifted so that she was straddling his lap, gazing down at him, her hands braced on his delicious shoulders.

His hands moved to her hips, sneaking under the tee-shirt she'd pulled on for comfort. "I mean, I want you to come with me."

Her heart pounded against her chest. Looking into his eyes, she could barely breathe, hoping that this...that he meant...! She didn't understand! "Why?"

He pushed a lock of hair out of her eyes. "Because I love you. And I suspect that you love me too. Because I want to spend the rest of my life with you. Because you make me happy. And because I love..."

He couldn't finish because Emma leaned forward and kissed him hard, tears streaming down her cheeks as she put all of the love she felt into that kiss.

When she pulled back slightly, he cupped the back of her head with one large hand. "Does this mean that you feel the same way?"

"I love you," she whispered. "I love you so much." She hiccupped, her hand flying to her mouth. "I love you, Rayed!"

"I love you too, but you still haven't answered my question."

She sobbed, nodding her head. "Yes!" she replied. "Yes, I'll come with you. I'll stay with you for as long as you want me."

"Forever, Emma!" he replied harshly. "This is a forever kind of thing." He gently tugged at her hair now, needing to see into her eyes. "I don't just want you to come with me, I want to marry you. I want to have children with you." He groaned, leaning his forehead against hers. "I want you to find all of the corruption in my government and expose it. Just as you've done here!" He shook her slightly. "Will you do that, Emma? Will you marry me?"

"Yes!" she replied, her hand flying over her mouth to stifle the sobs. "I thought you'd go back to Fahre and that would be the end of us."

"There is no end," he vowed. "I want you in my life forever, *habibi*."

She laughed again, nodding eagerly. He started to pull her closer, but she resisted. "Only if you tell me what '*habibi*' means."

He paused, dark eyes gazing into blue. Then he chuckled. "It means 'my love'."

Emma's soggy smile brightened, "Oh!"

"Will you marry me, Emma?"

Her heart pounded against her chest and she stared at him. For a moment, she thought about all of the things she'd have to leave behind if she married him. Her career, her apartment, she'd miss her friends, especially Amanda. But she'd gain Rayed. There was only one answer, "Yes!"

Epilogue

"Are you coming, woman?" Rayed called out, grabbing the remote for the television. "It's starting!"

Emma rushed out of the kitchen in their enormous private suite. They'd been married for three months now and every day was an adventure. Living in a palace with servants and a powerful man was... well, it was different. But Amanda was coming for a visit next month, after the book tour for her current murder mystery novel ended.

So far, life was pretty darn good.

"What are you doing?" Rayed called back, glowering at her.

"I had to add butter to the popcorn," she explained, sliding along the marble floors in her thick, woolen socks, balancing the huge bowl of buttered popcorn in her arms. "Has it started yet?"

She flopped over the back of the sofa, landing next to Rayed who grunted, then lifted her onto his lap. "It hasn't started." He tossed a handful of popcorn into his mouth. "Here we go."

Emma snuggled down, getting more comfortable and smirking when Rayed growled at her. She knew exactly what she was doing and laughed. But neither of them would do anything about the instant lust that ignited with her squirming. Not yet, anyway.

"And in recent news," the newscaster began, her expression turning serious, "Former Governor Mitchell was convicted of all charges this afternoon. In this video, you will see the former powerful leader as he tried to strangle his own lawyers after the jury returned with the guilty verdict. He was quickly restrained and hauled off to jail to await his sentencing hearing, which will be in two weeks. The former governor resigned months ago after the story broke that he was demanding payments from various state contractors in exchange for political donations, that he was manipulating internet markets and taking bribes from contractors in order to gain consideration for state contracts in low income neighborhoods. The corruption charges were first brought to the public's attention by reporter, Emma Giani, who is now married to Prince Rayed el Mitra of Fahre. Princess Emma, in a statement yesterday, explained that Prince Rayed was instrumental in helping her uncover the corruption of the former governor. The former governor hid his activities from the public by announcing outrageous, attention grabbing headlines that riled up parents and various organizations so that no one saw what he was actually doing."

The camera flashed to Doris Mitchell as she hurried out of the courtroom. Her head was bowed and she pushed a pair of sunglasses over her eyes, even though she was still indoors. But in that same moment, another man, a taller, more muscular man stepped close to Doris. And in that instant, Emma gasped as the man's arm moved around Doris' waist. An arm with a Dragon tattoo!

"That's him!" Emma asserted, pointing towards the television with a handful of buttered popcorn. "That's the man who pushed me down the stairs!"

Rayed's eyes narrowed, but the news station had already moved on to the weather report. He looked at her carefully. "Are you sure?" he demanded.

Emma leaned back, shaking her head. "No. I'm not sure. I only vaguely remember that dragon tattoo. And I don't have any evidence to prove that he's the one who pushed me."

Rayed growled. "I'm going to have my security team investigate. Now that we have a name, it will be easier."

Emma smiled at him, dumping the popcorn into the bowl as she leaned forward to kiss him. "You're amazing." Then something occurred to her. "And I think I'm going to convince Amanda to write a mystery novel about a man with a dragon tattoo on his arm. Maybe he's the one who wrote the note as well!" Emma's mind was moving fast. "What if she...?"

"You're amazing!" Rayed laughed, setting the bowl of popcorn off to the side and sliding his hands underneath her shirt. "However, I don't think that your idea of making the man into a mystery novel villain is enough for my sense of justice." He shifted their bodies so that Emma was stretched out underneath her. "I have some additional opinion about justice, my dear."

"So you think you can do it better than me?" she teased.

"Yeah," he laughed, moving his hand higher. "I think I can do it better."

Emma grinned in return. "Yeah. You know how to get things done, *habibi*."

Postlogue

Dillon Harbow dug through the disgusting smells until he found something edible. Lifting it to his mouth, he glanced around while stuffing the barely edible pastry that had been thrown into the dumpster the previous evening.

"Nice tattoo!" a guy that smelled like a urinal commented, hefting his filthy backpack higher onto his shoulder. "Dragon? Or some other mystical creature?"

Dillon muttered an epithet at the man and turned away, hurrying towards the darker end of the alley as he rolled his sleeve down over the tattoo.

His phone rang and he looked at the phone number. For three rings, he considered not answering the phone. But in the end, Doris was his only link to his previous world. "What?" he snarled.

"Dillon, where are you?" she hissed. "I have another job for you!"

Dillon looked around again, stuffing the rest of the donut into his mouth. "I'm still trying to get away from the goons."

She sighed. "Dillon, that was over a year ago. I'm sure that the security forces from Prince Rayed have given up on trying to find you."

"Think so?"

"I'm sure of it," she snapped.

"Yeah? So why did I barely escape from two of them this morning? They've been hot on my heels everywhere I go!" He ducked down behind another dumpster, his stomach growling. One donut wasn't enough to fill his gut. Plus, he needed some real food. "I've learned to live in the shadows ever since you suckered me into helping your pathetic husband with that last scheme. No way am I going to end up like your husband, lady!"

A movement at the end of the alley caught his attention. He looked at the phone, then at the two men that wore all black with large, loose coats. Since it was July, with temps in the triple digits, the coats meant that the men were concealing weapons.

"Did you do this?" Dillon snarled.

"Do what?" Doris replied, but the calm tone of voice warned him that the bitch had! She'd called him intentionally so that the men at the end of the alley could track his cell signal.

"You are going to pay for this!" he snapped, ending the call. He dropped the cell phone and crushed it under his heel. He wasn't going to be caught! Not by these men! Not by anyone! All he'd done was push a woman down the stairs and send one little threatening note! Now his life had turned into a nightmare where he was hunted down as if he were some sort of effing rabbit! The guards shoved something into their pockets, then walked pseudo casually into the alley. Dillon knew that he'd been found.

Looking around, he found a way out. It was iffy, but he reached up and, with all of his remaining strength, pulled himself up and over the brick fence. Some ass had embedded shards of glass into the mortar at the top of the fence, causing his hands and legs to be scraped, but he ignored the pain. Hopping down on the other side, he raced away. With a sigh of relief, he knew that he'd escaped being captured. Again. But how long could he do this? That damn Prince Rayed had sent a freaking army to capture him!

Never again would he listen to a woman! Never! And with that vow, he walked into the shadows.

A message from Elizabeth:

I know what you're going to ask me and YES – Amanda has her own story. Originally, Emma's roommate was only going to be a tangential character. But as I wrote the story, her personality developed in my mind and I knew that she had to have her own story. However, her romance happens in the Al-Bodari series. Her story is titled "His Impossible Heir" and comes out in December (so sorry for the long wait!). Go to you favorite retailer and preorder your copy. I hope that you enjoyed this story and that the ending didn't feel like a cliffhanger. I wanted the hunter's punishment to be that he was hunted for the rest of his life – like a backlash of Karma. Was the ending okay? Normally, I have the bad guys captured and put in prison. But I liked this ending better. Let me know if you didn't like the ending – or if you loved it. Or any other feedback. If you wouldn't mind, could you leave a review? Go to the book page on retailer site to the review page – and I thank you!

As usual, if you don't want to leave feedback in a public forum, feel free to e-mail me directly at elizabeth@elizabethlennox.com. I answer all e-mails personally, although it sometimes takes me a while. Please don't be offended if I don't respond immediately. I tend to lose myself in writing stories and have a hard time pulling my head out of the book.

Elizabeth

Want to read a short excerpt from the next book in this series? Keep scrolling for a quick look at Sada and Sheik Micah's story. It's a bit steamier than usual – but with a plot that will (hopefully) make you laugh and chuckle and sigh and roll your eyes.

Excerpt from "The Wicked List"
Release Date: March 10, 2023

"Yes!" she triumphantly whispered, then glanced around, embarrassed that she'd spoken out loud and praying that no one sitting in the crowded room had heard her.

Unfortunately, her eyes glanced to the hated man across the room and, of course, he was staring at her! In fact, the irritating ogre even lifted a dark eyebrow quizzically, almost as if wondering what had just occurred to her.

Ignoring him, Sada defiantly wrote down the next item on her "Wicked List". Skinny-dipping. Then as an afterthought, she added, "in the moonlight". Because what's the point in skinny-dipping during the daylight hours?

Oooh! That was a good one too! Was it more decadent to skinny dip at night or during the day time hours? She shivered, wondering what would happen if someone saw her skinny dipping during the daytime. Didn't matter, she added "in the daylight" down as a separate item. Why limit oneself? When dreaming, one should be daring!

She'd read a quote saying, "If your dreams don't scare you, they aren't big enough." That was her new mantra!

She even added an exclamation point to those two items. Flipping the pages back to her "official" notes, Sada calmly folded her hands and lifted her eyes, pretending to listen to the speaker. She really should be paying attention, Sada admonished herself with a heavy sigh.

Unfortunately, she'd completely lost the thread of the speaker's point. Sada knew that this meeting was important. All the regional leaders were in attendance at this conference. Sada was representing Fahre in her brother's absence. Her oldest brother, Tazir, Sheik of Fahre, refused the invitation, wanting to be with his wife, Lila, as they anticipated the birth of their first child. Rayed, the second oldest in their family, might have come, but Sada had convinced Tazir to reinforce his stance on women's rights by sending her instead of Rayed. Rayed hadn't fought for the "privilege" to attend, preferring to be with his new wife, Emma.

So, here she was, Princess Sada el Mitra of Fahre, triumphantly sitting in on the most tediously boring meeting in the history of meetings. The current speaker was droning on about...bridges? No, building materials. No...wait...Sada silently groaned. She had no idea what the man was lecturing about.

Her eyes moved over the other attendees and...darn it! *He* was still looking at her!

Sheik Micah al-Marri, Ruler of Batam. Fahre and Batam weren't exactly enemies, however, the two countries weren't exactly friendly either. The competition between Batam and Fahre was intense, both countries vying for prime business investors while their universities competed at research challenges. Their countries considered the competitions to be friendly and Sada knew that her brothers and Sheik al-Marri were on good terms. The men enjoyed getting together, either in Fahre or Batam, under the guise of promoting good will. However, Sada knew that the three men simply played poker and had a great time. They called it "on-going diplomacy". It was merely an excuse to beat each other at yet another competition and drink expensive alcohol.

Of course, all of the regional countries competed with each other. It was simply the nature of the world. Every country wanted to be the best at computing power, energy resources, technological advances, or whatever. But there always seemed to be a sharper edge to Batam's competitiveness. And Batam's ruler!

He was tall, she thought. Probably as tall as her older brothers, but since she'd always vacated the premises during their so-called diplomacy weekends, she'd never seen al-Marri standing next to either Tazir or Rayed.

And while her brothers were handsome in a rugged, don't-mess-with-me sort of way, there wasn't anything handsome about Sheik al-Marri. He was made up of lean, hard angles. Even his gaze was sharp and...! Sada gasped, suddenly realizing that she'd been staring at him and quickly pulled her eyes away.

Darn it! She didn't know the man, but instinctively, she didn't like him.

Another mischievous thought occurred to her and she flipped the pages in her notebook. Quickly, she scribbled, *"Have a man at my mercy."* Smoothing the papers down again, she turned her head, forcing her gaze back to the speaker. Dear heaven, this particular speaker's voice had no inflection to it. Glancing around, she noticed that the others were all a bit dazed, unable to pay attention when the speaker's voice was the perfect pitch for putting everyone to sleep.

Squirming in her chair, she tried to remain attentive. Reminding herself that she was the sedate, responsible, always polite sister, Sada lifted her eyes and forced her mind to pay attention.

Unfortunately, or perhaps because Sada was sick of being the *"sedate, responsible, polite sister"*, her thoughts kept drifting off to non-sedate, completely irresponsible, and outrageously impolite images. She wasn't just polite and responsible. Sada was also...completely inexperienced, she thought with a frustrated sigh. Sexually and in so many other ways. She hated that fact.

Everyone around her, all of her friends from boarding school and university were getting married and having babies. Or not having babies, not marrying, but living their fabulously exciting lives in the most outrageous and adventurous ways. She read about their thrilling escapades on social media or via the gossipy emails they each sent out to the group. Her friends were working hard at fascinating careers and playing even harder.

Meanwhile, Sada lived in a gilded palace, smiled politely for the cameras, wore demure dresses, and politely conversed with politically correct diplomats and world leaders. To the outside world, her life might appear wonderful and exciting. But here she was, surrounded by regional leaders, bored to tears, listening to someone drone on about the advantages of fabricated materials versus natural building materials, the tensile strength of...of...?

What in the world was tensile strength? And couldn't she just read an article about it and not have to listen to this monotone person? His voice would solve insomnia!

Suddenly inspired, Sada flipped the pages again, writing, "Scream with passion" as item number four. The speaker might not be conveying his message about...whatever...very effectively, but her "Wicked List" was shaping up nicely!

Speaking of wicked, her eyes flashed over to Sheik al-Marri. Sure enough, the obnoxious brute was still staring at her. Even as she watched, his thumb moved over his lower lip. Back and forth, his eyes holding hers without mercy. Sada felt her heartbeat accelerate and... had the room suddenly become too warm? She watched that thumb, suddenly mesmerized. What would it be like to have his thumb on her lip? Or even better, his lips on hers? Would his kiss be as hard as his image? Or would he kiss her tenderly? Was he coaxing? Or demanding? Both options seemed incredibly erotic!

As soon as she thought that last word, Sada's mind blinked back to reality. What in the world was she thinking? There was absolutely no possibility of her kissing *that man*! He was rude and obnoxious! How dare he stare at her during a highly important meeting!

Granted, she wasn't paying attention to the speaker either. But al-Marri didn't know that! Rude, obnoxious, horrible man!

Pulling her eyes away, she glanced out the window, wondering how long this horrible, tedious meeting would last. Surely this speaker was nearly done, right? Seriously, couldn't he read the room and notice that no one was paying attention any longer?

The sun was starting to set and she wanted out of here. She wanted to breathe in the fresh air and smile up at the moonlight, lift her arms up and feel the breeze on her skin.

Another idea occurred to her and Sada added *"Dance in the moonlight"*, then smiled. Her newest addition to her "wicked" list wasn't sexual as much as romantic and dreamy. Yes, she desperately wanted a bit of romance in her life.

However, she was trying to break out of her ladylike persona so she also added *"Sex in the shower"*. She'd read about that in a book and it had seemed really hot! She sifted through other sex scenes from the books she'd read and added *"Be on top"* as an action item. Shivering, she smiled.

Then Sada defiantly glanced over at Sheik al-Marri.

Sure enough, he was still watching her. She glared at him for a moment, silently conveying that she didn't appreciate his attention! But the dratted man merely lifted that dark eyebrow at her as if silently asking, "What are you going to do about it?"

Bastard, she thought in annoyance.

Sada flipped the pages again and underlined *"Scream"*. Yep, Sada was wretchedly sick of being silent. She was tired of protecting everyone else's feelings by keeping her mouth shut. Sada wanted to scream, rant, and voice her opinions. She wanted to stand up and tell the idiot man still blathering on about...whatever...to shut up!

And yet, she remained politely in her seat. Because of the frustrated emotions roiling inside of her, she pretended to write something in her notebook. The speaker said something about sand and glue and...she wrote all of that down, as if it were an ingenious idea.

Finally... the speaker concluded his comments. After a moment of polite applause, the audience jumped up, obviously eager to get out of the room. Thankfully, this was the last meeting of the day. There would be a formal dinner tonight and then the regional conference would be over. Everyone would return to their countries. The participants would grant interviews to reporters. They would rave about how innovative, how congenial the conference had been, and how eager they were to implement the ideas in their countries and build new relationships. Blah, blah, blah.

Sada grabbed her belongings and stuffed them into her leather tote bag, relieved to get out of this chair and away from the speaker. Oh, and she was intensely relieved to get away from the too-knowing gaze of an obnoxious ruler with insufferable eyebrows and a thumb she fantasized about breaking.

Sheik Micah al Mari watched the beautiful Princess Sada hurry out of the meeting room, transfixed by the gentle sway of her shapely hips and long, graceful legs. Unfortunately, he could only see her calves because of the stiff, black suit she was wearing, but...hell, they were great calves! Slender ankles, strong muscles, and...unfortunately, that was all he could see of her legs.

She'd distracted him during the meeting and he was fascinated by the various expressions that had crossed her lovely features. Her lips were lush and full and he could picture her doing amazing, shocking things with those lips. His body stirred, just picturing those "things". And her eyes! Her body language feigned a demure appearance, but her eyes flashed with fire. Every time she looked at him, he could see that fire, the passion, anger and desire in those eyes. Micah was captured!

If he'd been the marrying kind, Micah would have been tempted to contact her brother, Tazir and ask for...what? He wasn't the marrying kind. He'd visited Tazir and Rayed over the years, but their interactions had focused on diplomacy and poker. Sheik Tazir was a tough, but fair, ruler. Perhaps Tazir would be more receptive to an offer of marriage. It would be a good alliance, Micah thought as he watched her escape through the double doors to the conference room.

The only problem with that plan was that Micah wasn't the marrying kind. Yes, he should probably produce an heir. But that wasn't going to happen. Love and marriage was for other people. He didn't believe in that love-crap and there was no possibility that he would allow himself to be trapped into a political marriage. Not even for a pair of soft, brown eyes and a great pair of legs.

Several other leaders interrupted his view of the woman and Micah focused on the short conversations. He shook several hands and nodded his agreement about whatever they were talking about. But with the double doors open, he had a clear line of sight to the woman standing just outside the perimeter.

"Your Highness, I'd appreciate your opinion about..." Micah wasn't listening but he must have made all of the appropriate replies because the man in front of him kept speaking, unaware that Micah's eyes kept shifting over the man's shoulder to the lovely woman.

Princess Sada continually drew his attention. He wanted her. She was a gorgeous woman and...hell, that mouth! He'd love to know what it was like to kiss a woman with lips like hers! He'd love to see her thick, dark hair down too. Hell, he'd love to weave his hands into that cloud of hair, gently tug her head back so that he could expose that long, sexy neck, find all of the places on her neck that made her moan or shiver. He'd love to...!

His body warned him that his thoughts were going to become obvious soon if he didn't focus.

Made in the USA
Monee, IL
09 February 2023